**"Get aboard the starship, Lara"
said Jor-El.**

"No," Lara replied, "As your wife, my place is with you. The ship will have a better chance of escaping Krypton's gravity without my weight. We must give our child, Kal-El, a chance to survive. Remember we named him 'star child' in ancient Kryptonese."

"An accident of language. Get on."

"I am a Kryptonian woman, and Krypton is dead. I must remain here."

Her refusal did not surprise Jor-El. He pulled a prepared recording disc from a shelf and slipped it into a slot on the navigational unit. It would have to serve as Kal-El's introduction to the distant planet that was his destination.

"My dear God," Jor-El whispered as the rocket carrying its tiny burden lifted off amid the crashing of metal and rock. "May the starwinds guide your course, Kal-El."

And the vacuum of space muffled the star child's wailing as a giant world ripped itself apart.

SUPERMAN
LAST SON OF KRYPTON

by
ELLIOT S.
MAGGIN

WARNER BOOKS

A Warner Communications Company

WARNER BOOKS EDITION

Copyright © 1978 by National Periodical Publications, Inc.

All characters are trademarks of and © DC Comics Inc. 1978

All rights reserved

ISBN 0-446-82319-8

Warner Books, Inc., 75 Rockefeller Plaza, New York, N.Y. 10019

A Warner Communications Company

Printed in the United States of America

Not associated with Warner Press, Inc., of Anderson, Indiana

First Printing: December, 1978

10 9 8 7 6 5 4 3 2 1

The scribe recorded the words of Sonnabend the prophet. Words that would be preserved for eternity by the immortal Guardians, a collection of verses to guide the righteous across the eons.

Not for billions of years, by Earth measure, would the words of the particular verses he now recorded apply. But when the time came, they would certainly prove true:

> Star Child will leave a deathworld
> For the System of the Rings,
> Where the child will grow to legend
> As his life the singer sings.
>
> When the conqueror wants his secret
> With the Star Child he'll contend;
> And when day of battle's over
> Then the legend's life will end.

As he recorded these particular verses a small shudder rattled the time around the scribe. . . .

1

Krypton

He'd tried. God knew Jor-El had tried. But the end would come sooner even than he had thought. Probably before the sky over Kryptonopolis turned red with daylight one more time. Only a superman could finish pounding together the family-size starcraft before stresses at the core of the planet splattered Krypton across the galaxy.

Since two stranded space wanderers found each other on the big red planet ten thousand star orbits before, the world had been in its death throes. In geological terms it had been enough time to draw a final breath. In human terms it had been over seven hundred wildly successful generations. Enough time to build a prosperous, self-satisfied civilization. Enough time to grow proud of a race that had tamed a world so unfit for human life that early generations had to sleep more than half the day and felt more comfortable crawling on all fours than walking erect. The gravity was that intense.

If ever in the history of the galaxy there had been a

test of survival of the fittest among the human family, it was on Krypton. The weak died before they could produce offspring, yet the infant mortality rate was frightful for thousands of years. But here, as on the thousands of other more habitable worlds across the stars to which man had migrated, the human species displayed its surprising adaptability. The land changed man long before man changed the land.

The race's physiology was subtly altered while outward appearances changed very little. Muscle tissue became denser. Motor reflexes became sharper. Perceptions broadened. Optic capacities widened. A whole new range of physical abilities began developing, just to allow human beings to live under normal conditions on a planet whose gravity was monstrous, whose weather changes were drastic, whose sun was unusually variable as to heat and generally too dull as to light intensity. Finally, when the suffering was near an end, when subsistence on resources of a near-depleted planet became possible, the race of humankind began to spread north and south from the relatively low-gravity equatorial regions, and the humans began to build.

They built with a vengeance, these tuned-up humans. With vengeance, and ruthlessness, and a good deal of bloodshed. To begin to build on Krypton they had to hack ruthlessly at jungles of rock-tough vegetation and forests of molten lava. They had to do what worked—fast. Those who do not let nature stand in their way do not allow other humans to do so, either. In building, as in adapting, the primary rule was to survive.

Once a civilization began to come together on Krypton, humans began to turn their attention to values. Among the creatures of the Universe humans possess a relatively high capacity for good. The Kryptonians took as an assumption of their lives the fact that there was a right and a wrong in the Universe, and that value judgment was not very difficult to make. To kill, for example, was wrong. To give somebody food, for example, was right. Through generations of slavery, warfare, and of human sacrifice in the name of progress, the population of Krypton ached inwardly for tranquillity.

The humans of Krypton became tranquil too soon. That was to be their downfall.

Given that there is a right and a wrong in the Universe, it is easy to conclude that the death penalty imposed by those in authority upon those who commit terrible crimes is wrong. When the Kryptonian people turned their attention to polishing off their hard-won civilization with values, capital punishment was one of the first things they abolished.

Criminals were, as a rule, a troublesome group of people. The problem was not that they were difficult to apprehend, but that they were quite a bother to keep both alive and away from law-abiding society at the same time. Jor-El first came into prominence as a scientist by devising a method to do that.

Barely finished with his education, young Jor-El presented his "phantom zone projector" to the stodgy group of gentlemen who governed Krypton, the Science Council.

Now, instead of putting convicted criminals into suspended animation and shooting them into orbit around the massive planet, a less costly and far less troublesome practice was instituted. Jor-El postulated a plane of existence on the border of his own, and he devised a method to enter it. His theory was correct. So now criminals were chained to a wall and exposed to a phantom zone ray. They were, in entering this borderworld, effectively reduced to non-corporeal form and made to serve their sentences as ghosts, able to witness events but not influence them.

Jor-El found the gates of Hell—and this was what gave the young man access to the Science Council. Someday, it was said, Jor-El would chair that council.

For some time Jor-El was a rising star among his fellow Kryptonians. His mind was the marvel of his age. Heir to a long line of scientists, inventors, explorers, and public administrators, he grew up listening to his father, the industrialist who popularized mass production, his mother, a prominent social activist, his uncle, the inventor who found the first practical uses of geothermal energy, and an older cousin who was a great spiritual leader talk about the future of Krypton as if the world were a social laboratory of unlimited possibilities. The young man was never led to suppose that anything within the realm of the human imagination was impossible.

No one on Krypton had ever possessed the talents for theory as well as technical application that came so naturally to Jor-El. After the phantom zone discovery, Jor-El designed and built a prototype family-size traveling vehicle on three wheels which could be produced cheaply and was powered by Krypton's nearly limitless supply of thermal energy. Following close behind that accomplishment was the intelligence analyzer, a device that could measure the activity of a waking brain and determine the level of the brain's development. It measured the natural ability of a newborn child as well as the success of the individual in taking in information through his period of education. Jor-El's own quotient, of course, was beyond the device's ability to measure, as was that of his wife Lara. Even Jor-El, however, was taken aback by the reading he got when he exposed his infant son Kal-El to the analyzer.

There were dreams of space travel running through Jor-El's mind. The only viable power source on the planet was Krypton itself, where turbulent forces at work below the crust produced heat that could be effectively mined and harnessed. For space travel, Jor-El was convinced, the solution was understanding the fields of gravity that held the Universe together. He had visions of starships sailing gravitational winds between the stars at speeds approaching that of light. Jor-El was toiling over figures and data trying to design a unified, coherent gravitational theory when he chanced upon some alarming information that conventional modes of thought as to the nature of the planet could not explain.

It was over three years before the event took place that Jor-El discovered Krypton would explode. He had first made his announcement in secret to the Science Council.

"I think young Jor-El is scared of a few groundquakes," Vad-Ar the Elder said, expressing the general view of the councilors.

The Science Council, along with the great majority of the Kryptonian people, had grown soft and complacent. They had tamed a harsh world, these humans, and now it was time to relax and enjoy their accomplishments.

Let anyone suggest that these accomplishments would soon be swept away in a single fit of cataclysmic fury, and he would be laughed at. Let anyone persist, and a public mockery would be made of him.

As far as the public was concerned, it was a buffoon, a crackpot sick with overwork who stood welding plates of alloy into the hull of the starcraft through this restless night. Birds and insects flew this night, herds of animals stampeded across ground never to be subjugated by humans. They knew. And men still laughed at Jor-El.

"Jor-El. What are you doing?" The scientist's young wife Lara stood in the doorway of the workshop wrapped in a housecoat. She carried Kal-El, their son, in her arms.

"We're going to have to leave before dawn. Go back to bed and let me finish this thing."

"Jor, I woke up when I heard the baby crying and I

11

found myself alone. Now I find you in here, telling me we're going to leave our planet—our *planet,* for the love of all that's holy—before dawn. You want me to go back to bed?"

"You have the choice of sleeping or winding yourself into a frenzy. If you choose the latter, I suggest you do it somewhere else, because it will only hinder my work." Jor-El didn't look up from his tinkering.

"You've already worked yourself into a frenzy, Jor. And you've lost your perspective because of it." The infant in Lara's arms began to whimper.

"Go back to bed, woman." Jor-El snapped on a pair of goggles and picked up a liquid mortar burner to weld.

"You may have observed that women have not been at their husbands' command for several centuries now. And if you turn on that burner while I'm talking, you may also notice—"

He turned it on and Kal-El began to cry at the sudden noise.

Lara was about to turn off the geothermal generator from which the burner drew its power when a tremor shook the burner from Jor-El's hand. Before the burner hit the floor the generator was dead. The tremor had severed the generator's line to a power source below the surface of the planet.

"Damn!" Jor-El glanced toward the makeshift launching rig already set up in the open bay window of the workshop. "Look out there, Lara. The spire over the Science Council chambers is toppling."

"I hear crashes from all over. What is it, Jor?"

"You'll soon hear screams in the streets as well. Put the child down and help me set that prototype craft on the launcher. I wouldn't have finished the big ship in time, anyway."

"But that little thing—it's only big enough for one person."

"Two, if they squeeze a bit. Give me." Jor-El gruffly took the howling infant from Lara and placed him on a workbench.

"What do you think you're going to do with this toy, Jor?" Lara helped him set the seven-foot prototype starcraft on the rig at the window.

"Send you and the child into space. Here, let me get that navigational unit off the big ship's nose."

"No, you're not."

Jor-El ignored her and went about fixing the little silver navigational mechanism to the tip of the child's craft, ready to separate and eventually fly several light-hours ahead of the main unit.

As he did that, Lara found two musty blankets in a closet. She wrapped the red and blue blankets around the infant, who was already struggling in a yellow sheet.

Jor-El finished a few final calculations and turned to his wife. "Get aboard, Lara."

"My place is with you. The ship will have a better chance of escaping Krypton's gravity without my weight, anyway."

"Your place is wherever you can survive—and that isn't here."

"Remember what we named our son, Jor? Kal-El meant 'star child' in ancient Kryptonese."

"An accident of language. Get on."

"No. I am a Kryptonian woman, and Krypton is dead. Give the child a chance."

Jor-El wasn't surprised, only disappointed. He pulled a prepared recording disc from a shelf and slipped it into a slot on the navigational unit.

"My dear God," Jor-El whispered as the rocket carrying its tiny burden lifted off amid the crashing of metal and rock. "May the starwinds guide your course, Kal-El."

And the vacuum of space muffled the star child's wailing as a giant world ripped itself apart.

2

The Fiddler

The old man was growing weary of fiddling. The only reason he was spending this fallow time tugging on his bow was that his nurse had hidden all his pipes and he wanted to do something with his hands. Once he was in a string quartet, but all the members were gone now. Once before that, in the old country, he had appeared on stage in a great music hall and played some of his favorite melodies, and the public adored him. The next day a review full of sumptuous praises was published in the newspaper, and he clipped it out.

"Look here. Look at this," he would tell friends as he pulled it from his billfold. "I'm not what you think I am. I'm a famous fiddler."

Maybe if he had practiced more as a little boy that is what he would be doing for a living today. Maybe he would be happier. Then again, his belly would probably not be as full. He certainly could not take issue with the life the Fates had handed him. There were those he had loved in his way, and his accomplishments appeared considerable enough. If only people wouldn't treat him as if he were brittle as an eggshell. For example, what he wanted now most in the world—even more than his pipe—was an ice cream cone. As his bow caressed the strings he began formulating fanciful plans for sneaking out to the ice cream parlor before the nurse knew he was gone.

"*Herr Doktor*," the nurse called, "your mail is here."

"Is there anything important?" he asked as she breezed into the bedroom.

"The Dean of Faculty mentioned yesterday that this one would come. It's a request that you speak at the freshman banquet next month. It's only a formality that he asked you. He doesn't expect you to accept."

"Freshman banquet? You mean the first day of the school year?"

"Yes, they have one every year."

"I have not met a freshman in years. I believe I would like to go."

"*Doktor,* it would certainly be an unnecessary strain."

"Strain shmain. What else is there?"

"Something from Mr. Ben-Gurion. Probably a thank-you note. All the rest look to be from children. I'll open them and send your picture to the ones with a return address."

"Won't you leave them here? I think I would like to read some mail from children today."

She did, and the old man flipped a tuft of furry white hair from his face with the bow and resumed playing. For a moment he thought there was a slight buzz in his superb violin. Unthinkable. But as the hum got louder he realized it was coming not from the instrument at all, but from the window behind him. He turned to see what it was, and sitting on the open window sill was the oddest-looking mechanical device he had seen all day. Beyond the window, rolling by on Mercer Street, was a collection of teenagers in a 1939 DeSoto convertible. He decided the device was the second-oddest machine he had seen all day. He changed his mind again when the thing addressed him.

"I have sought out, through this device, the greatest mind on this planet to tell you that an event will take place in a short period of time which will concern you as well as the rest of your world," were the words he heard.

There was an odd intonation of the words. They seemed all to run together, and yet he heard them with exquisite clearness. As he approached the machine, the words became neither louder nor softer. They were constant. Very interesting, he thought, as he considered what this visitor might be. Then he realized that he could not tell whether the machine was speaking German or English. He drew some conclusions.

"Pardon my simplicity," the old man said, "but have I the honor of addressing God?"

The machine resumed its announcements as if in answer. "My name is Jor-El and I am speaking to you through the use of a device which relays spoken information directly into the mind of the individual it contacts. My recording is incorporated into a navigational device whose purpose is to lead my son Kal-El to a planet inhabited by intelligent creatures whose thought patterns roughly correspond with those of the humanoids of my planet, Krypton. By the time you receive this message my world will have been long destroyed by natural forces. Since that cataclysm, my infant son has been traveling through space at a speed close to that of light, and the time has passed for him slowly enough so that he is just beginning to feel the effects of a day without food. At this moment he is slowing down in preparation for entering your field of atmosphere."

This was too fantastic. The doctor's mind raced over possible methods for one of his students to have set up this prank. He put his hands tightly over his ears and still heard the words perfectly clearly. He played his violin and the sounds of the music seemed on another level altogether. What he was "hearing" from this machine was not sound. Could it really have been a telepathic recording?

"Just as the navigational device was drawn to a world of intelligent beings, it was drawn to you, the most highly developed intellect on your world. The purpose for this is to implore you to take in my son Kal-El as your own and see that he is raised to proper manhood."

The possibilities of this being a hoax were quickly being eliminated in the old man's mind. He was listening intently.

"My son is of a highly developed humanoid species. Legends of the creation of our world imply that we are an offshoot of another world somewhere, and that at some time many worlds were seeded with humanoids. This is why I hold out hope that you yourself may be one. It would matter little, however, if you were not, as long as my son was exposed to the proper intellectual stimulation during his upbringing. I will attempt to pinpoint the location of Krypton in relation to the course my son's small rocket traveled and in that way enable you to determine where and when he is likely to touch down on your world. . . ."

And the old man scurried to his desk and notepaper, almost excited. He would get past the nurse today, but not to buy an ice cream cone.

3

Smallville

He was not a small man, though he looked slight and shambling as he hunched in his seat on the bus. But now he was standing, a little stooped, next to the driver with one hand grasping an airline bag and the pole to keep steady as the other hand groped through the pockets of his baggy pants for change.

"Thirty cents," the driver said.

"Just a moment. Right here."

The old man's German accent touched off the driver's memory of the loss of a brother in the Second World War not long ago, but the wrinkled man smiled through his mustache as he maneuvered a handful of coins toward the tips of his fingers. There was something familiar about that smile.

"Here we are," and the old man dropped a quarter and a dime into the driver's palm, "thirty cents."

The driver didn't move to make change, since the old man seemed not to notice it was due him. The guy might have a nice smile, but a nickel was a nickel, after all. The driver might have wondered why he tugged his woollen cap down over his ears on a day as warm as this, but he wasn't that observant.

"Excuse me, officer." The old man stopped a policeman in the charming rural village. "Do you know of a nice hotel maybe?"

"Yes, sir, at that corner you make a right for a block and you'll see the Smallville Hotel sitting there big as life. Staying in town long?"

"No, just a day or so. Thank you, officer."

"Visiting friends? Relatives?"

"Yes. Friends. Thank you very much."

"I'll walk you there, it's just down the block. I'm Captain Parker. George Parker, Mr.—"

"Eisner. Umm, Calvin Eisner. Lovely day, no?"

"Certainly is. Rained yesterday, though. Where are you from, Mr. Eisner?"

"The east. New Jersey. Tell me, is there a taxi company in Smallville?"

"Sure is. You can call them from the hotel. Free direct line. What do you do in Jersey?"

"I teach. I am a teacher."

"A teacher. I love kids. I thought of being a teacher. Couldn't afford college, though. Who you visiting in town, if you don't mind my asking?"

"Who? Umm, whoever it is that owns that ice cream parlor over there. I haven't had a good ice cream cone in weeks. Would you join me in an ice cream cone, Captain Parker?"

"Seems a long time to go without ice cream. You been out of the country?"

The old man wondered whether the policeman was simply being friendly or whether he recognized him. The tight woollen cap hid the distinctive flurry of white hair, and the fact of being in a totally unlikely place, he thought, served to complete the disguise. It did not occur to him that with four years of the kind of paranoia that war brings about, it might be hard for the officer not to be suspicious of someone with a thick German accent. It was necessary, though, to meet as many people as he could in the next several hours, so he treated Captain George Parker to an ice cream sundae and checked into the hotel as Calvin Eisner.

In the hotel room he pulled the cap off and jiggled his head until his scalp could breathe. He sat on the bed, cupped his hands under his chin, stared out the window, and thought of Krypton. There were images, not only words, in the message from Jor-El. Images of a giant world circling a great red star. This world was huge, and not a gaseous, amorphous mass like Jupiter, but heavy with rocks and minerals and incredible gravity. Yet there were people there, walking and talking a completely foreign language, and living day to day in much the same way as those on Earth lived. This child on the way from that world would be quite an individual, born on Krypton and raised on Earth. The mere physical effects the change in environment would have on him would certainly be considerable.

The youngster would be human, the old man decided, that was for sure. But he would be a tuned-up human, a Kryptonian.

The old man imagined what it would be like to have muscle tissues heaped one on top of the other and ground together as hard as the composition of matter whose subatomic particles had fallen in on each other—to have a sun that makes normal skin tan make your supersensitive skin indestructible—to have every sensory nerve ending stimulated all the time—to be constantly aware of your environment's every aspect, every quirk—to be able to hear for perhaps as great a distance as there was a sound—

conducting atmosphere—to see for incalculable reaches of space—to be able to negate even the tug of gravity with your own finely tempered mass.

He imagined this, and then imagined growing from infancy in that state. Being able to develop your motor reflexes through a body designed to weather terrible wear before it reaches maturity. Growing inside that body in surroundings that nurture rather than hinder. He imagined to what ends such massive excesses in physical and freed-up mental capacity could be turned with the proper guidance. Imagined approaching the upper limit of human potential.

The old man was never one to shrink from the wondrous and terrible places his analytical mind could take him; that was the source of his greatness. These thoughts, though, gave even him pause. There was every possibility that today the Earth would become home to a superman.

The old man considered the immense possibilities for disaster that might accompany such an event. There were, of course, even greater possibilities for benefit, and it was only now beginning to dawn on him how squarely the responsibility for providing conditions favorable to those benefits fell upon his shoulders. There was work to be done.

It seemed amazing, as he walked onto the street with dusk beginning to fall, that he had received his mechanical visitor only about nine or ten hours earlier. Now, how did one meet people in Smallville?

Unfortunately, Smallville was apparently closed. It was a dry town; that was a good sign. The only place of business he found open was a small general store on Main Street where he bought a local newspaper, a corncob pipe, and some tobacco, all of which he enjoyed immensely until he fell asleep in his hotel room.

Morning was brisk, and the heavy woollen cap that hid his thick hair was almost comfortable. The old man was beginning to wonder whether the inquisitive police captain, George Parker, was his man. He was friendly, probably honest, had a secure job and was waiting outside for the old man as he shambled out of the hotel.

"Top of the morning, Mr. Eisner."

"Captain. What a pleasant surprise."

"You mentioned you needed a taxi, and I thought since I was in the neighborhood I'd offer to take you where you're going."

"Well, how considerate."

"Where was it you were going, now?"

The man huddled under his heavy sweater and drew on his corncob pipe. He was starting to notice a hint of suspicion in the policeman's disarming manner. "Actually, I was planning on taking a walk this morning. I would like to see what your lovely town looks like. Can you join me?"

"Walking around Smallville is what I do for a living."

"You keep long hours, Captain Parker. How does your wife feel about that?"

"I'm a widower. The force is about all I've got right now. Hope to be police chief someday."

"Oh, I am sorry. I lost my wife, too, some years ago. A man should have someone who can take care of him."

"Suppose he should. But I do all right."

The child should have a mother. Parker would not do.

"Surely you have other interests, Captain. Hobbies?"

"Oh, not really. Used to go sailing a lot, though. Tell me, Mr. Eisner, just who was it you wanted to—"

"Sailing? I love sailing. You know, I have my own sailboat. I go out every week on a lake where I live. Did you know that at the time of Columbus people did not even know how to sail into the wind?"

"Do tell?"

"No one had ever thought of something as simple as tacking with a rudder. Can you imagine that? One would think perhaps da Vinci or Archimedes or someone could have come up with the idea with not much effort, but no."

"Maybe we could go sailing then, before you leave Smallville. How long did you say you would be staying?"

"Perhaps we could, Captain, that would be nice. Do you have a boat?"

"Not one of my own, but Sam Cutler here rents them by the day. The fella that owns the hardware store over there."

It was not simply a hardware store. There was hardware sold there, but also used heavy farm equipment, lumber, building supplies, and the finest collection of small sailboats the old man had seen in a long time. One in particular, a nine-foot Ketcham-Craft, drew his attention, and Parker wandered into the store after him when he insisted on measuring its dimensions.

The old man interrupted a conversation the proprietor was having with a handsome middle-aged couple to ask for a tape measure. "I know Franklin Ketcham, the sailboat racer," the old man whispered to Parker. "I had no idea he had gone into manufacturing."

"Sure is a fine-looking piece of machinery, Sam," the middle-aged man was saying to the shopkeeper, "but eight hundred for a used tractor is a little out of my range just now."

"For you, Jonathan, seven seventy-five."

"You make it look awfully good."

"Jonathan," the woman piped up, "if we can't afford eight hundred dollars, how can we afford twenty-five dollars less?"

"I don't know, Martha. Twenty-five dollars is twenty-five dollars, like the man says."

"Sure it is, Martha," the salesman insisted, "and look at that trailer attachment back there. See how solid it is?"

"Little rust underneath, ain't there?"

23

"That's not rust, Jonathan. That's weathering. Gotta expect a little weathering, don't you know? That'll haul twice as much as any horse you ever heard tell of."

"We sure need a tractor, Sam, we sure do, but I don't want to go into debt for more than another five hundred if I can help it."

"What's your worry, Jonathan? The war's over. We won. The country's depending on the farmers like you. Come here and look at this transmission."

The old man was chuckling with glee as he wrapped the tape measure over the hull of the sailboat. "That old goniff!" he mumbled at the policeman.

"Old what?"

"Crook. That old crook."

"Sam? Can't blame Sam, he's honest as the next guy," the Captain snorted. "Just that Jonathan and Martha aren't to be believed."

"He used my design. Every inch of it."

"Every panhandler in town knows Jonathan Kent's a soft touch. You just can't help taking advantage of his good nature, but I'm not one to talk."

"He told me he was trying to design the perfect recreational sailboat, and he showed me all his figures, and I did a little sketch on a napkin and here it is."

"A shame they never had any children. Maybe it's just as well, he never made any money with that farm of his."

The old man looked up. "What did you say, Captain?"

Captain Parker wondered if it was time he started being overtly suspicious of the eccentric man with the German accent. Parker thought better of it when Eisner unceremoniously injected himself into Sam Cutler's sales pitch.

"I could not help noticing that you were looking for a tractor, Mr . . . Kent?"

"That's what I'm here for."

Blasted jerry, the shopkeeper sneered to himself.

In the next five minutes the old man convinced Jonathan and Martha Kent that he had a tractor deal for them that could come only once in a lifetime. You see, he explained, family responsibilities had forced the old man to sell his farm and go east rather suddenly, and he had a brand new tractor, next highest model after the one the Kents were looking over, for just five hundred dollars.

"Well, I'd sure like to look at it, Mr. Eisner," Jonathan Kent threw the bemused Parker a wide grin, "but Sam here's nearly got me convinced on this one."

"If it's everything Mr. Eisner says it is, we should surely look at it," Martha Kent insisted. "I'm sure Sam would understand, and we don't have to take Mr. Eisner's if we don't want it."

The old man directed the Kents to meet him and the tractor at a certain place outside Smallville at precisely six-fifteen that evening. Not a minute sooner or later.

Outside the hardware store, Parker cornered the old man. "Listen, pal, anyone who goes out on a limb like that for a perfect stranger is all right in my book, but who are you, really?"

"I believe I will have to trust you to keep a secret, Captain Parker, though I must caution you never to reveal I was here. I cannot tell you why."

"Let's hear what the secret is before I agree to keep it."

"That is not the best of conditions, but I will need your help."

The old man pulled off the woollen cap and shook free his shiny white hair.

Parker's face registered his stunned recognition. After a speechless moment he said simply, "Welcome to Smallville, sir."

4

The Tractor

By noon James Morgan Stone had had three tranquilizers and four cups of coffee. The first cup of coffee was to wake him up when he came to the bank in the morning. The first tranquilizer was to calm him down from the effects of the coffee. The second cup of coffee was to counteract the work of the tranquilizer. And so forth. Stone was president of the Smallville branch of Heartland Bank and Trust Company, and the only bona fide drug addict in town. If he did not have his curious mixture of caffeine and tranquilizers for a day he would be unaccountably bedridden and would often catch a bad cold. He had never spent a vacation in entirely good health, and for this reason he had not taken a vacation in over ten years. This was why, five years earlier when Stone was thirty-eight, he impressed his superiors enough to be appointed the youngest bank president in the state.

Stone's father, Alexander Hamilton Stone, had also been president of this bank. Everyone remarked on how like his father the younger Mr. Stone was. The older Mr. Stone died of stomach ulcers at the age of fifty-three. The younger Stone could now easily pass for a man in his late fifties.

When Captain Parker walked into the bank, followed by the disheveled old man in the ratty sweater, Stone was doing a fine job of looking dignified as he pretended to go over the previous day's transactions. Someday Stone hoped to be president of a bank that had a private office for its president so he did not have to appear diligent for the amusement of his employees. He was considering his next tranquilizer.

"Jimmy, wonder if you could do us a favor here." Parker was standing over Stone's desk. Policemen and politicians were the only people in Smallville who presumed to call him anything but Mr. Stone or Sir.

"Captain Parker, good morning. What can I do for you?"

"Mr. Eisner here would like to take out a short-term loan, y'see—"

"I'm sure Miss Brackett over there will see to you. If you'll excuse me."

"We'll, it's not your normal everyday loan, Jimmy, if you know what I mean."

"I have no idea of what you mean. Perhaps you could explain yourself to Miss Brackett."

"I doubt it. It's sort of a third-party loan. Mr. Eisner is from out of town and he has no collateral and I'd like to back up his security, or whatever you call it."

"Well, have a seat, I suppose." The old man and the policeman sat down opposite Stone. "Now, how much did you say you wanted to borrow, Mr. Eisner, and for how long?"

"Two thousand three hundred dollars, for just a few days," the old man answered.

Stone glanced at him over his glasses, hearing the accent for the first time. He weighed down his prejudice with his crisp manner. "What sort of identification do you have, Mr. Eisner?"

"I don't have any."

"What is the money for?"

"I would rather not say."

"Do you have any references in Smallville other than the Captain here?"

"No, I don't."

"What are you smiling about, Parker?"

"I was thinking that your expression is about the same as the one you had in high school when Martin Lang asked for your vote for Student Council president."

The old man's eyes twinkled, and Stone's ears turned red. The memory of his ignominious defeat for the student government post by Lang didn't bother him so much as the reminder that he had ever been an insecure, gawky, acne-ridden adolescent in Smallville at all. He wished people would simply accept the exalted position he held today and not remember the fact that he was not born middle-aged.

"This loan is out of the question, Parker. I'm sorry, Mr. Eisner. Now, if you'll please excuse me."

"That's what I thought he'd say, Eisner. Sorry I couldn't do much for you."

"No, no, no, Captain. Don't get up." The old man put a hand on the policeman's shoulder as Stone surreptitiously popped a tranquilizer. "I still need to you to co-sign my loan. Mr. Stone, I wonder if I could call a bank in New Jersey to confirm that my account will cover this amount?"

"There is a public phone over there." Stone pointed without looking up from the records he wasn't reading. "The word over the phone of an out-of-state bank official is hardly valid collateral."

"I know. May I have ten dimes for a dollar?"

"Teller's cage."

Parker sat smiling in a way that nearly annoyed the urbanity out of Stone. The banker tried in vain to think of some way to let Parker know that whatever the secret was, Stone wasn't interested.

The old man stood talking on the pay phone in the corner of the bank for three minutes. Then he shuffled back to Captain Parker and asked if the policeman would like to be treated to an ice cream cone down the block. The two left, and Stone's next trip to the coffee percolator was interrupted by the ringing of his private telephone line. He sat at attention when he heard the voice at the other end.

Four minutes and seven seconds after Parker and the old man sat down opposite a corpulent pair of sundaes, the bell over the door tinkled, and in walked James Morgan Stone flashing a keyboard of teeth.

"What kept you, Jimmy?"

"Kept me? Nothing kept me. I just thought I would join you gentlemen in a snack. I have good news, Mr. Eisner."

"How delightful. I love good news."

"The bank has decided to grant your request for a loan immediately, for whatever terms you specify."

"Yes?"

"Well, isn't that good news, Mr. Eisner?"

"Good, yes. News, no. May I buy you a sundae, Mr. Stone?"

"Oh, no, much too fattening. I have to watch my health. Just coffee for me. Black."

On the way out of the ice cream parlor Stone dropped behind and tugged at Parker's elbow as the old man stepped out the door. "George," Stone hadn't called Parker by his first name since high school, "George, who is that man? Who did he call from the bank before?"

"I 'spose he called his bank back home."

"Like fudge he did. Do you know who called me the moment you stepped out?"

"No idea."

"The president of Heartland Bank and Trust. The big man himself. He said he got a call from the Chairman of the Federal Reserve in Washington and that I was to give Calvin Eisner whatever he asked for. Do you believe that? The man in charge of printing up American currency and distributing it issued an order to grant the loan. Who is he? FBI? CIA? The President's secret agent?"

"Couldn't tell you. Maybe he's the President in disguise. Wouldn't that be a kick in the head."

"Come on, George. You know who he is. I can tell from the way you acted in the bank. What does he do?"

"Let's just say he's a national monument."

At the bank the old man whistled Bach's *Brandenburg Concerto* Number Two as he stuffed two thousand three hundred dollars in hundred-dollar bills into his little airline bag. Parker kept a hand on his revolver as he accompanied the old man to the police car and drove him to a tractor dealer in a nearby town. Parker had never seen anyone pay cash before for anything bigger than a Victrola.

"Good gosh, Martha! Did you see that?" Jonathan Kent nearly swerved his pre-war Oldsmobile off the dirt road as a ball of fire boomed across the sky.

"That's the biggest shooting star I've ever seen, Jonathan, and it isn't even dark yet. Do you suppose it could be . . . something else?"

"Like what? Another one of your Communist plots? Looks like it landed near here." The middle-aged man's eyes lighted with childlike glee at the prospect of finding a meteorite so close to his farm.

"But shooting stars don't crash like thunder. Jonathan, don't—"

"How do you know? You ever been this close to one? Look, I can see it smoking. Right beyond that bend where the tractor's supposed to be." Kent coughed his car into third gear and the ancient machine loped up like a hyperactive moose.

"Oh, Jonathan, what could you possibly want with a rock from the sky?"

"Some rock!" Jonathan and Martha Kent screeched to a halt ten feet from a smoldering seven-foot missile that had cracked several trees beside the road. It was now perched with its nose on the ground and its tail resting on a half-felled trunk.

"Be careful, Jonathan. It could be dangerous."

Jonathan wasn't careful. He hopped out of the car and easily pulled open the hatch of the craft. He stared for a moment as if focusing his eyes.

"What is it, Jonathan? What are you looking at?" Martha Kent was still in the car.

"I think it's—it's a baby." And the child immediately began to yelp at the top of his lungs.

"A—" Martha Kent ran toward her husband, who was jolted by the volume of sound coming from such a tiny creature.

"My land, Jonathan!" Martha Kent reached to pick up the baby from the craft. "The thing looks about to explode. Let me get the poor child out of there."

The craft began to hiss, and Jonathan Kent's eyes widened. "Get behind the car, Martha! Quick!" he shoved the woman away after she'd barely had a chance to look at the infant in her arms.

He pushed her behind the car and huddled with her and the baby as the thing they had thought was a rock from the sky screamed like a thousand busy telephone wires, crashed in on itself and vanished in a blinding burst, leaving only the fallen trees as evidence of its presence. A note on the tractor parked a few feet away asked Jonathan

Kent to send five hundred dollars to a certain bank in New Jersey whenever he had the chance.

About fifty miles away a long black limousine sped eastward along route 46 carrying two terribly competent young men in pinstriped suits and a grumbling old man in a ratty sweater with a mane of white hair flying in more directions than could be counted.

"Bars all around me," the old man complained. "I should have stayed to see what Hitler would do with me. At least a concentration camp has people to keep me company."

"Terribly sorry, sir."

"I can't smoke my pipe because they're afraid I'll lose my breath. I can't go on a trip because they're afraid someone will hit me over the head with a picket sign. I can't go for a walk some days because it's too cold or too hot or too nice out. God forbid I should catch a cold; people with advanced medical degrees specializing in whichever nostril is stuffed come swarming to my home like a horde of mosquitoes. It's enough to keep me healthy until I'm sick of it."

"Your nurse was very worried, sir."

"I shouldn't have made that telephone call. You would think three minutes isn't long enough to trace a call."

"Our equipment can do it in under two minutes now, sir. Why were you in Smallville, anyway, sir?"

"That I'll tell you when the Messiah steps out of a flying saucer onto Times Square doing an Irish jig."

Not long afterward the old man stopped playing the violin. In the next several years he would become fascinated more and more with his work. He would never retire. He would be touched and honored with offers of the presidency of a great university and of a promising new nation, both of which he would decline with regret. He would always continue to receive letters from children. In 1955 the old man would pass away in Princeton, the town that gave him a home for his last twenty-two years. The world would mourn his death. He would certainly be remembered and revered for centuries to come.

5

The Anchorman

Years of wonder and terror came and went, years of multi-media and future shock. Of Camelot and War of Attrition. Men walked on the Moon, and women marched in the streets. Economic and social institutions fell with the sounds of rolling thunder, and self-proclaimed prophets rode private jets to preach of an end to material values. Cities of silver towers raked at the sky like wire hairbrushes and ancient lakes went stagnant and dead and the world was afflicted with a hero.

Among the monoliths in the city of Metropolis stood the Galaxy Building, housing a communications network that reached a greater percentage of the world's population than any spoken or written word since the Voice of God told Adam it was time to wake up on the morning of the sixth day. Here in Metropolis were the theaters and the film companies, the advertising agencies, the publishers, the design and garment manufacturing centers, the think tanks and universities, the ideas, the energy, the vitality that drew young men and women from thousands of miles around to grab at a piece of their own particular dream. One of the young men who came to Metropolis was Clark Kent of Smallville, to study journalism at Metropolis University, to land a staff reporter's job at the *Daily Planet* and later to become local news anchorman at WGBS, the flagship television station of the Galaxy Broadcasting System. The bespectacled Kent was tall, dark, and inoffensively handsome. His face could be broadcast to millions of viewers each day, and he could walk through midtown crowds without being recognized by a living soul.

Morgan Edge, the president of Galaxy Communications and wundkerkind of the network television industry, "discovered" Clark Kent when Galaxy bought the *Daily Planet*. Edge reassigned Kent to television news, and it was not until two years later that it occurred to the executive that newspaper experience made Kent capable of doing more than reading aloud the words written by someone else. So besides being anchorman of the local evening news, Kent was associate producer of the show. This made it his responsibility to see that available reporters and crews were assigned to the right stories and to decide what news was to be covered in the daily hour-long broadcast. It also meant that Kent had to be in the newsroom before anyone else, going over newswires and trying to figure out in mid-morning what the news would be by the end of the day.

"Hey, Clarkie, what's news?" Steve Lombard, the sports broadcaster and former first-string quarterback for the Metropolis Astros, lumbered into a newsroom full of clicking wire service receivers and clacking typewriters. "Get it? What's news? Ain't anybody got a sensa humor around here?"

"Good morning, Steve." Clark smiled as he tried to figure out whether he should eliminate a story about a twelve-year-old girl swimming across Long Island Sound in favor of a nineteen-year-old engineering student who had equipped a Volkswagen to run on twelve storage batteries instead of gasoline.

"Ah, good old conscientious, punctual, enterprising, dull Clarkie. Can't you say anything besides 'good morning'?"

"Nice day, isn't it?" The engineering student had a distracting tic when he talked. Clark decided that for television the little girl was more newsworthy.

"Same old faces around here," Lombard muttered. "Same old routine. Boyoboy, when they told me I was gonna be on the tube every day, I figured the chicks'd be climbing the walls like King Kong to get next to me."

"They're not?"

"Well, I 'spose they are. But there's something missing, know what I mean, Clarkie?"

"What do you mean, Steve? Love? Affection? The sort of thing that makes lasting relationships, right?"

"No, I got all that. Maybe I should grow a mustache."

"What've you got lined up for your spot today, Steve? Isn't this the day you do an on-the-air interview with Pelé?"

"Yeah, hey, hey!" Steve cuffed Clark on the shoulder, and Clark fell back clumsily, more out of concern for Steve's hand than anything else. "Guy can sure kick that soccer sucker, hey, Clark? Get it?"

"Got it."

"He'll be here about four-thirty. Great guy. Had a Bloody Mary with the dude last night at the Ground Floor."

"He broke training?"

"Nah, the season ended last month. You gotta keep up with the news, man. This waitress—y'know, Maureen, the one with all those low-cut drinks—she kept coming on to

35

him, y'know, just to be nice 'cause he's a friend of mine."

"Couldn't be she liked him, could it?"

"Sure she liked him."

"How do you know?"

"She told me when I dropped her off at work this morning. Why's the place so dead today?"

"Had to send a lot of crews on the road."

"Slow news day in town, eh? 'Smatter, old Musclehead ain't helped any old ladies across the street with super-breath lately?"

"I guess there hasn't been anything spectacular for him to do the past few days. Maybe he's worried about Luthor's escape last week."

"Luthor, huh? He's been in the headlines since he broke out again and nobody's seen hide nor hair of him. Pretty hard to see a hair of him. Get it?"

"As long as the FBI issues statements that they expect an arrest within twenty-four hours, we've got something to say about him."

"Ah, that bald fruit's not human. Third time he's broken out this year, ain't it?"

"Fourth, if you count last New Year's Eve."

"Everyone knows the FBI's not in Luthor's league. We're just waiting for another showdown between Baldy and the Super-guy, right?"

"I suppose, but Superman doesn't issue a press release every day, so we go with what we've got."

The people of Metropolis were secure enough in their big-city provincialism to look up when they heard the high-pitched wind-tunnel sound in the sky no more often than they looked at the tops of the buildings around them. But there were still the tourists on the crowded streets who responded when some lunkhead yelled, "Look! Up in the sky!" Someone would always answer, "It's a bird!" and then a few people would yell, "It's a plane!" and in a boom of voices that was more often than not louder than the whistling wind in the sky, "It's *Superman!*" Then again, few were the natives who had been out of town for some days who did not find themselves joining in the chant and then swelling with territorial pride under their button-down collars.

Superman was a public phenomenon without precedent. No other public figure, even in the golden age of monarchy, ever so excited people's imaginations almost from the time of his birth. From the fanciful reports of a flying baby in a red-and-blue playsuit twenty and thirty years ago, to the public appearance of a teenaged Superboy from a lost planet, to the conferring of international citizenship on Superman by the United Nations years ago, this alien had become the most famous man on Earth. If a news show had lots of Superman film, it became popular. If a magazine had him on the cover, it outsold everything else competing for rack space. If he made a public appearance, the locals talked about it for years.

Children played in imitations of his red cape. He made skin-tight outfits, especially in red and blue, a recurrent fashion among men not generally given to fads. The symbol he wore on his chest, a stylized *S* in a symmetrical irregular pentagon, was the most widely recognized trademark in the world. His crusade against crime, his awesome feats to minimize natural and man-made disasters, inspired millions of people to enter crime prevention, conservation, medical research, and similar fields. He could fly under his own power, he was strong enough to juggle planetoids, indestructible enough to take a steam bath at the core of a star, and he had the ability to see through most solid objects and to hear for unlimited distances. No other human could do what Superman could do. Every other human aspired to be him. He brought with him the birth of an age of humanitarianism on Earth; he reawakened the hope for peace. There were those who said there was a dark side to his presence, as well.

By lunchtime Clark Kent's blackboard in the WGBS newsroom was nearly filled with assignments. Tricia Felins was downtown with an auricon crew filming a piece on the safety of schoolyard playgrounds in the city. Johnny Greene was covering the Mayor's press conference on drug rehabilitation programs. The Mayor was bucking for a Senate nomination and Greene was bucking for a post as the new Senator's press secretary. Jimmy Olsen was sixty miles away with a videotape crew at Princeton University's Institute for Advanced Studies, covering the opening of hitherto unseen documents left in a vault nearly thirty years ago by the late Professor Albert Einstein. Being processed in the lab was a three-minute "Plant Spot" feature about how to cope with an indoor coleus that grew big enough to take over the room. Already in the can was a special six-minute film in Cathi Thomas's series on the artists who were living in the converted lofts of an area of Metropolis that was once a crime-ridden eyesore. Three young reporters were running up enormous phone bills double-checking the authenticity of the hard news coming in from around the world via Associated Press and United Press International. Oscar Asherman was on the Galaxy Building roof playing with his barometers and anemometers like a child fascinated with an Erector set. Steve Lombard was in a corner, feigning ignorance of the English language in order to have an excuse to enlist Janet Terry, fresh as peaches out of Columbia School of Journalism, to help him on copy to accompany sports footage. By lunchtime Clark Kent's daily wrestling match with the *WGBS 6 O'Clock Evening News* was largely won, and Lois Lane was on her way up from the sixth-floor offices of the *Daily Planet* for their lunch date.

The bell rang twice on the Associated Press wire, not enough to cut into programming with a bulletin, but significant enough for the associate producer of the city's major local news show to get up from his typewriter and see what was up. As Clark held up the rolling yellow sheet of paper and watched the story type itself out he saw Lois step out of his office down the hall and he waved at her.

"Hey, Clarkie, what's popping?" came the voice from the same direction as another swat to his shoulder. "Well well well, willya look at who's prancing down the hall dressed to stop a convoy. Heavy lunch hour, Clark?"

"Oh, Lois? Guess so." Lombard seemed to smell the lady approaching at three o'clock out of a cloud like a World War I ace. "Weren't you showing that new girl Janet how to write to film, Steve?"

"She'll be all right in the editing room. She's a fast learner. Hel-loooo, Lois."

"How's it hanging, Grizzly?" Lois stepped in the hallway door. "What're we doing for lunch, Clark?"

"Oh, I thought maybe Patty and Brew or—"

"Yeah, Clarkie." Lombard tried hard to look as genial as a hibernating polar bear. "What're we doing for lunch? Taking a Lear jet to Paris for hors d'oeuvres? Morocco for beef curry? Dessert in New Oreleans?"

"Get off it, Grizzly. You know the last time Clark had a comeback for a one-liner he fell off his moa."

"Lois! Isn't anyone on my side?" Clark's exclamation was only in his words. He seemed never to rise above a conversational tone or a walking speed.

Steve Lombard was another matter. Lois had long ago stopped feeling guilty about the amusement she felt when she watched the two men together. She realized that there was no point in feeling guilty because Steve seemed, under it all, quite as incompetent as Clark at human interaction.

Like now, for example, she allowed a creamy grin as Steve waved a hand, talking and trying to distract her and Clark, as he used the other hand to slip the corner of Clark's jacket—it apparently never occurred to Clark to take off the jacket indoors—into the roller from which the two-alarm story was emerging. What would happen next, Lois thought, was that as Steve tried to turn the crank, pulling Clark's jacket into the machine and making him look stupid, a fire bell would ring and Clark would jump away in time, or a light fixture would fall on Steve's head, or the big boss Mr. Edge would walk in and yell at Steve for horsing around or—

As Steve leaned back to yank at the handle and mangle Clark's suit, the crank picked that moment to fall off in Steve's hand and leverage left the quarterback sprawled on the floor in a pile of discarded wire copy. Unflappable, Clark Kent ripped off the current message, about a swarm of hang gliders seen approaching from the outskirts of the city, and dropped it on Steve's face.

"Gotta go eat, Steve. Would you have somebody check out this story while I'm gone?"

"Nuts!" The sportscaster flew to his feet and down the hall ahead of Clark and Lois. He bumped into a cute young copy girl on her way to the newsroom and snarled, "Who're you?"

"Laila. Laila Herstol, I—"

"Shouldn't be working on your lunch hour. My treat."

"Really? Sure, Mr. Lombard."

"Look at him, Clark. One after the other. You think he collects scalps, or puts notches in his shoulder pads or something?"

"Don't know, Lois, but someday he's liable to injure himself."

What no one had noticed was that the crank of the Associated Press ticker had not broken. It had melted. Clark would cover up the fact the first chance he got.

Patty and Brew was a quickie lunch spot half a step over McDonald's and Burger King in exclusiveness. Both male and female heads turned Lois's way as the pair walked the block to the restaurant. There was no denying the lady's striking appearance, and it went well with her brisk, almost manly stride. She had been on the talk show circuit for years plugging one book or another, and then there was the perennial gossip about her and Superman. Hardly anyone who looked noticed she was with a man, much less that the man was Kent. She was the show on this block.

That was, until a faint whooshing sound came from the sky. Pedestrians froze, and traffic slowed, as people craned their necks looking for a red-and-blue streak. But what they heard was the distant beating of police helicopters and what they saw were half a dozen of what appeared to be hang gliders, propelled by tiny jet engines and rotors. One of the gliders left formation and hovered over the Metro National Bank and almost instantly a low-pitched rumble shook the ground.

"Luthor!" Clark spat.

"What?" Lois said. "What are those things?"

"High-pitched sound coming from devices in the gliders. Probably at exactly the pitch that will shatter tempered steel. As in bank vaults."

"What? Clark, how do you know all that?"

"My nose for news."

"Is there a cliché you haven't hit yet today?"

"Look, Lois. You stay and watch what happens. Take notes. I've got to get a film crew on the roof for the show, anyway, so I'll let Perry know you're covering the story for the paper."

"Oh, no, Clark Kent. You've stepped on enough of my bylines, and the old man would hop at the chance to get your name over a front-page story. I'll call my editor myself, thanks." Lois elbowed into the restaurant and its public telephone.

By the time Clark had had the chance to smile at his own cleverness he slid into the lobby of a building that was emptying quickly. Once he found a corner safely away

41

from onlookers he moved faster than any eye could follow. The glasses, the blue jacket and pants, the tie, shirt, and shoes peeled away in a twinkling. A curl of blue-black hair dropped over his forehead.

And for no more than another instant there stood the most powerful man on Earth.

6

The Penthouse

Yesterday Luthor was dressed in skin-tight pajamas and crossed ammunition belts. The outfit was the only affectation he had for a purpose, and therefore the only one he recognized as an affectation. The penthouse hideaway four hundred feet over the city, the medieval tapestries hanging over the faces of the computers and wall consoles, the Egyptian sarcophagus whose mummy was replaced by a mattress covered with Snoopy sheets and pillowcases, paintings on the walls by Leyendecker, Peake, Frazetta, and Adams, those weren't affectations. Those were matters of taste. Luthor was flying in the terrace window with his jet boots for the seventeenth time, and he was running out of videotape.

Six videotape recording units operated by six wanted criminals stood at different angles facing the pathway from the terrace window to the far wall. "We're going to get it right this time," Luthor said, "then we work on the disappearing shot and we're into the projection room for splicing and recomposition into a holographic image. It's going to be a long night."

Nobody groaned. This was the highest-paid staff in organized crime.

Lex Luthor firmly believed in the theory that there was some Universal law yet unexpressed by the temporal humans who lived on Earth, which explained the clashes of great opposing forces. When the United States teetered at the brink of collapse, a socio-political genius named Lincoln appeared to steer the potentially disastrous forces in the direction of positive reform. When Caesar began to amass dangerous power, Brutus found the moral strength to stop him. When armies of procreating hominids of various states of development began to overrun the habitable areas of the Eastern Hemisphere and compete with each other for food, there arose *homo sapiens* with their wheels, their tools and their weapons to subjugate the land and take the future for their own. When a super-powered alien brought his hyperactive sense of propriety across the heavens in order to cram it down the gullets of perfectly capable, sentient Terrans, there came Luthor, a creative marvel who alone among the human community was capable of keeping that self-important, cape-waving pork-face in his place. Luthor saw himself, as he saw Lincoln, Brutus and the inventor of the wheel, to be an integral part of the inexorable eddies and currents of the Universe. He was a product of natural law.

For every social force, Luthor thought, there is an

equal and opposite social force to balance it. Maybe that was the Universal law he had in mind. Maybe it was that simple. In one of the hundreds of biographies of the man that Luthor read before he was old enough to balance an oxidation-reduction reaction, he found that Einstein would approach each new problem of physics the same way. Evidently the old man would sit back in his chair, close his eyes and ask himself how he would arrange the Universe if he were God. When Lex Luthor now asked himself the same question he came to the inevitable conclusion that his rule about the balancing of social forces was true. Everything is in or approaching a state of equilibrium. There is no good and bad, no right and wrong, no Heaven and Hell. There is not even any middle ground. There is just dead center.

Therefore, Luthor had to do all he could to make life difficult for Superman. Not to do so was equivalent to trying to repeal Ohm's Law or Pauli's Exclusion Principle. It was Luthor's duty to the Balance of Nature.

Luthor now saw, with hindsight, that it was inevitable for his life to be bound up with that of the Kryptonian almost from the day Superboy began to exercise his power on Earth. The notice on page three of the four-page *Smallville Times-Reader* about the Luthor family taking title to the old house on Merriellees Lane was in the first issue in that publication's history in which the editor, Sarah Lang, chose to decorate page one with a banner headline. The headline read:

ARMY TO INVESTIGATE
SMALLVILLE ANGEL

The so-called Smallville Angel was how the written press across the country accounted for a series of apparent miracles that were happening in Smallville with increasing frequency over the months immediately preceding Luthor's arrival there. Children in the process of drowning would suddenly find themselves waking up by the side of the lake; furious tornadoes would regularly unwind and sputter out on the edge of town; thieves cruising away from the scene of the crime would find themselves stopped short, surrounded by neat little jerry-built cages made of tree trunks or mud or whatever was handy—cages which vanished as immediately as they appeared when the police happened upon the scene; that sort of thing.

Everyone in Smallville knew by this time that there was no angel. People had caught glimpses of the little boy in the red and blue flying suit for years. He would be in his early teens now, and the people of Smallville generally felt that it was time the outside world took notice of their Superboy. Everyone who walks the Sierras knows the day-to-day habits of the legendary sasquatch. Every New Englander who lives north of Manchester, New Hampshire, knows there is a lot of flying hardware in the sky from somewhere other than here. Every half of a pair of identical twins knows what telepathy feels like. No federal commission has to put a label of legitimacy on reality. It is always nice to think, though, that government officials have some concept of what reality in fact is.

Superboy seemed to come to the conclusion that if the army wanted to see him, there was no reason he should go out of his way to hide himself. The week Jules and Arlene Luthor, their teenage son Lex and their infant daughter Lena moved into the house on Merriellees Lane, there appeared the second banner headline in the history of the *Smallville Times-Reader:*

SUPERBOY REVEALS HIMSELF

and the three words filled the entire first page under the paper's logo. The special expanded issue was eight pages long, carried no advertising, was completely devoted to the subject of Superboy. There was a complete transcript, for example, of the dinner conversation at the White House where the President honored the young hero, but there was no room for the fact that a new family had moved into town.

Luthor thought it was significant that the local weekly newspaper never did get around to recognizing his family's presence. As it turned out, the family would not be in Smallville for long.

Young Lex Luthor's first happy memory of Smallville was a minor flap he caused by turning out to be the top science student in the eighth grade. This caused some excitement because Lana Lang, the red-headed daughter of the woman who left the Luthors out of the *Smallville Times-Reader,* got the idea that for some reason Superboy had another identity. She thought that he was probably one of the boys in the eighth grade. Lex's quiet appearance in town at the same time as Superboy's spectacular revelation, as well as the new boy's uncommon brilliance, prompted the insufferably cute little girl to follow Lex around like a puppy for the better part of a week. She thought he was Superboy and the new kid appreciated the attention.

Lex was a touch bored by schoolwork. He did not much like following direction, but he liked to experiment, especially in his chemistry class where he found a lab partner with pretty much the same attitude. Lex and his lab partner had an assignment one day to demonstrate in front of the class how two deadly poisons can be combined chemically to make a nutrient which is actually necessary to the human body. Lex and his partner had to combine sodium with chlorine to make table salt, and then sprinkle it on a scrambled egg and feed it to everyone in the room. Lex had had breakfast before he came to school that morning and thought the idea was going to be a thundering bore, so before he left for school he stuffed a fake plastic scrambled egg from a novelty shop and a few jars of chemicals from his father's workshop in the basement into his coat pocket.

It was Lex's job to combine the chemicals while the class watched, his lab partner's to scramble and fry three eggs over a bunsen burner in an aluminum camping frypan. Lex rigged up an inverted cone and clear glass tube over his reaction to distill the salt and keep any excess chlorine from escaping into the room. Then he looked over at what his partner was doing. He grimaced.

"Hey, that's no way to scramble an egg."

"Whuh?"

"Lookit that. Egg juice all over the place. Yuch."

"What do you mean egg juice?"

"All over the top. You have to stir it around a little so it all gets cooked."

"That's the way my mother makes it."

"Listen. Your mother ain't a great cook just 'cause she's a mother. Mine burns water."

Everyone in the class laughed at that except the lab partner, who didn't get it. "How does she do that?" he wanted to know.

Lex knew his lab partner was too bright to be that dumb, but the two had a good act. Lex had a straight man. He ran a finger of water into a beaker, held it in one hand and waved the other hand over the top like a good stage magician. Lex was sure his partner noticed the micro-milliliter of substance he sprinkled over the surface of the water from his waving hand, so that when he brought the bunsen burner near it the water seemed to pop into flame.

Lex was also sure that his partner noticed, when the rest of the class was distracted by the flame, as Lex switched his fake plastic egg with the chemical compounds under it for the real scrambled egg. His partner was a good kid and didn't let on. Sometimes he was too good.

So when Lex took the plate of fake egg out from behind the lab table, held it out to the class and sprinkled his sodium chloride catalyst over it, a big black glob of smoke

47

flung itself from the dish like a dragon bursting from the sea. Lex howled. Both he and his lab partner got detention for a week. Years later, when Lana Lang told the story, she swore the burst of smoke had claws.

Young Lex had curly brown hair, a nose he thought was too long, and big feet that tended to point outward instead of forward when he walked. Little kids took to him the moment he grinned, older people seemed unable to resist the urge to pinch his cheek, boys his own age hated him as soon as he opened his mouth in class for the first time, cute little red-headed girls made him stutter and occasionally choke when he tried to talk to them. When Lana Lang saw Lex and Superboy at the same time —the hero showed up in time to smother a potential explosion in a chemistry experiment Lex was trying one day when his lab partner was absent—the girl lost any interest in him. When after a few weeks Lex turned out to be not only the top science student but the top math, history, English, art and French student as well, the only kid who made any effort to be Lex's friend was his lab partner, Clark Kent.

Lana Lang was the second-to-the-top English student. Clark was second in everything else. Luthor decided that Clark kept his friends by being the eighth grade's top nerd. Lex would rather keep his dignity. Clark Kent grew up to be a mindless mouthpiece for some petty fiefdom in the American Corporate Empire. Lex Luthor built an empire of his own.

Yesterday, Luthor tromped out to the terrace. A moment later the man behind one of the taping units called, "Rolling!"

Lex Luthor, resplendent in purple and green, collar raised, sashes holding vials and bizarre weapons, small jets in his boots belching flame, flew into the room cackling like a rabid hyena. He waved in front of him a rolled-up leather folder as he burst in, did a pirouette in midair, bounced gracefully off the wall with both hands and feet, and hopped to the floor as he snatched back his composure and said, "Cut!"

"Think we've got it?" the boss asked his six cameramen. They all thought so.

"All right, take your places for the next shot."

That was yesterday.

7

Princeton

"Slow down, boy," Jimmy Olsen told himself for the fourth time since he got up this morning. He said this to himself out loud when he was bored, frustrated or excited. This time it was the first. The reason he told himself to slow down when he was bored was that he tended to get worked up over the fact that he had a dull assignment today, and he probably would not get to show off his go-get-'em, let-'em-have it, boy-wonder reporting on the air. He had dazzled the world yesterday and the day before; he would probably do it again tomorrow. At twenty-three Olsen was the youngest on-the-air reporter in Metropolis. He was also probably the most worried about his career.

Jimmy Olsen found himself orphaned and alone at sixteen, supporting himself as a copy boy for the *Daily Planet*. By eighteen a series of freelance news stories written on speculation earned him the position of "cub reporter." By twenty-one Perry White, the paper's editor, had made him a full member of the *Planet* staff. Beside being an electronic journalist, now he wrote a feature column for the Planet Newspaper Syndicate three times a week. Somewhere along the line Jimmy picked up a high school diploma from the back of a matchbook, led a South American safari to locate his father who had been sitting in the jungle for years with a form of amnesia induced by malaria, learned to operate every newsgathering gadget from the typewriter to the WGBS-TV newsvan, entered the *Guinness Book of Records* for being thought killed in the line of duty more times than anyone else in any profession, became world famous, and convinced himself his life was headed absolutely nowhere.

A few more days like this one, covering the opening of a vault holding a notebook written by a man dead twenty years, and someone might sympathize with Jimmy's frustration. Jimmy thought of himself as the last of the Vikings, maybe a direct descendant of Leif the Lucky and Eric the Red. He certainly had the hair and complexion for it. So he was only five feet seven, nobody's perfect.

The Institute for Advanced Studies in Princeton was a nice place to put a housing development. It was said that Albert Einstein himself designed the layout of the place. Some layout. One brick baronial mansion housing the Institute, surrounded by a parking lot, a lawn the size of six or eight football fields and a hundred or so acres of woods which were punctuated by circuitous walking paths stretching for miles but leading back approximately to where they each started. The great man used to spend hours, days plodding over these paths trying to figure out exactly what gravity was. Jimmy could have told him. It was the stuff that kept the Australians from falling off the Earth. Jimmy had learned that from the back of a matchbook.

It was a little after eleven in the morning when Jimmy, his cameraman, and his sound technician pulled up in front of the Institute. The "camera" was actually a video-tape recorder and needed no sound man, but try to convince the union of that. The only people in sight were half a dozen other reporters, two camera crews, and a few college students walking dogs on the big lawn.

"Hey, man." Jimmy motioned to a reporter in a turtle-neck shirt and an awfully obvious rug on his head. "Anybody tell you when this show gets moving?"

"What?" He jumped.

"Seen any eggheads around? When do they open the safe?"

"Oh. Noon." The guy was terse.

"Then why'd I get up so early?"

He shrugged.

"I'm from WGBS. Who're you with?"

"Philadelphia Enquirer."

"The *Enquirer*. You know Evy Wuener? She's on staff there now, isn't she?"

"I don't know her. I'm new."

"Should meet her, man. Girl's got the best pair of typing hands this side of Poughkeepsie. Tell her Jimmy Olsen says hi."

"Sure."

Jerk, Jimmy thought. All those middle-aged guys struggling to write a lead paragraph for some backwater rag were jealous, that was it. Well, so the *Enquirer* wasn't a rag. So why didn't this guy want to say more than half a sentence to a colleague who was a legend in his own time? And who cared, anyhow?

At a quarter to twelve a little man in a tweed suit appeared at the main door of the building. Jimmy scribbled in his notebook: More teeth than Carter—sleeps in his suit—academic type born at the age of eighteen.

"I wonder if you'd all be so ki—uh, nice as to co—uh, step into the Inst—uh, the building here."

The notebook: Needle scratches on his larynx.

"I'm Mist—uh, Doctor Donald Ackroyd. Any questions, gent—uh, ladies and gentlemen?"

The guy from Newark, of course, wanted to know if there were free drinks for the press. Jimmy remembered his asking the same question at that Alcoholics Anonymous convention last year. Creep.

Apparently no one knew what Einstein had left in this vault. Everyone figured it might be pretty valuable or the greatest genius of the twentieth century wouldn't have gone to all the trouble of locking it away for twenty-five years. Geniuses were pretty weird guys, though. People thought Luthor was a genius, and no one ever knew where he was coming off. And Superman had to be a genius. Talk about crazy lifestyles. A secret fortress carved out of a mountain in the arctic; everybody said he dressed up as a normal guy during the day and went around sniggering at people who couldn't fly. All the time chasing after gangsters and flash floods and waving at the tourists. If Jimmy were a super-powered alien, he thought, he wouldn't waste time piddling around on Earth. There was a Universe out there.

Notebook: Three armed guards—one to open the vault and two to look tough—lotsa spooky guys with dark glasses and bulging lapels—taking no chances.

The guy from Newark ogled the girl from CBS. The fool from Philly with the wig hung from a corner snarling at the world. People got out of the way when Jimmy wanted his cameraman to get a closer look. It's great to be a star.

The guard in the middle pulled open the door of a vault about the size of a refrigerator. Before anyone could get a close enough look to see if a light went on when the door opened, out flew Lex Luthor, cackling like a bad dream.

Jimmy was the only one who kept his head. That was the way it always worked. He elbowed past the reporter with the eyeballs hanging out of their sockets, hopped over Dr. Ackroyd who was on his way to the floor, grabbed the .38 out of the shoulder holster of the plain-clothesman who was screaming, and let loose two shots in the direction of Luthor's cue ball head as the criminal passed through the wall like smoke through a window screen, waving a rolled-up leather folder—the treasure from the vault.

A few composures caught up to Jimmy's as the laughing ghost did a midair pirouette on the other side of the window. Jimmy led everyone—reporters, cameraman, officials, guards—through the door. Now some of the spooks had drawn guns and were firing at the jet-powered thief.

How did he get into the vault?

How did he pass through the wall?

How can he be so sure of dodging the bullets?

Why did he want the Einstein document?

Only Jimmy's cameraman was recording this. Every station in the country would pay a mint to get copies of that tape. The students on the lawn came running into the melee. Their dogs all galloped off into the woods.

Luthor waved his prize in the sky. Jimmy dropped the gun and grabbed his microphone.

"The door of the vault seemed open not even enough for a man to pass through the crack when Luthor scrambled out over the heads of reporters, waving the priceless papers and laughing louder than life. He went through the wall of the Institute like a ghost, and as you can see, instead of leaving the scene he swings back and forth in the sky like a man on a trapeze—"

Good simile. Wouldn't need much editing.

"—as if defying Institute guards to pick him out of the air like a clay pigeon. Ladies and gentlemen, what you are witnessing—"

Jimmy felt more like a ringmaster than a newsman.

"—is the daring theft by the greatest criminal scientist of our time of the last artifact from the life of possibly the greatest scientist of all—uh—oh."

Just as Jimmy felt the words rolling, he choked off. Luthor faded from the sky, along with his booty, as if he had never been there, and the guards were left seeding the clouds.

At that moment, the toupeed man who said he was from Philadelphia was slipping out a back door of the emptied Institute building carrying a soldered lead case the size of a geography textbook. Luthor tore off the fake hair as he plopped into his confederate's car, laid the sealed document on his lap, and headed for the New Jersey Turnpike.

The vault door hung wide open with nothing beyond it but a small empty table and the glow of a single 40-watt bulb. No one would be surprised to find Luthor's fingerprints all over the tiny room.

8

The Power

Nobody heard the whistling in the city sky until it was all over. This was business.

There were three gliders still in formation, heading in a wedge over midtown. Nine more were at a standstill fifteen to twenty feet over the roofs of nine major banks, each hovering under the power of a trio of small rotors on the points of the triangular kites. Waves of infra-sound beat downward from little plastic boxes on the pilots' legs. The one-man craft were masterpieces of simple design and fuel conservation. There was only one technician in the world with the talent and resources to design and build a squad of them. The pilots of the vehicles wore heavily padded outfits along with helmets that had a small monopole antenna over the left ear. Police helicopters—four of them—beat onto the scene with loudspeakers blasting.

"Attention—land your craft on the roof of the nearest building—"

The three pilots in the three gliders still soaring toward their respective destinations laughed. They were the Queen's clipper ships against the Spanish Armada. They rode stallions while the police chased on the backs of dinosaurs.

"No charges will be pressed if you debark immediately—"

One of the three glider pilots banked left toward the Banco Internacionale building. His vehicle vanished and he found himself hanging eighty feet over the sidewalk, and he told himself he was going to die.

"If you do not cease unauthorized activity within ten seconds—"

The doomed pilot looked at the spinning sky and saw that the pilots of the two other gliders in his formation were following him down and their gliders were nowhere in sight. He looked down and in the time since he last saw the ground a huge red cloth had been stretched over the street with two corners tied around two lampposts.

"You will be fired upon—"

plop-plop-plop

The pilot fell on the red cloth, and the two others followed. He was alive. The cloth gave way like a trampoline. He rolled across a red valley, felt himself bump into one of the other pilots, and tried to get to his knees. He felt nauseated.

"You have ten seconds—"

He saw the far ends of the cloth and what was holding onto the corners there. The man in blue. He felt the surface below him give way like a beach blanket as he was thrown by an irresistible wave against the sky and several times the pressure of normal gravity mashed his face in.

"—starting NOW!"

Superman calculated that the force with which he flung the three men into the air put their initial velocity at 160 feet per second. They would rise 400 feet into the sky and it would take them five seconds going up and five dropping back down. These thoughts flew through his head as he untied the corners of his red cape from the lampposts and fastened the clips inside his shirt as the cloth snapped back to its normal size. And the helicopter loudspeakers filled the air.

"Nine seconds."

Superman directed a narrow blast of air between his two front teeth. A block away one of the three rotors keeping the glider stable began to spin too fast. The front end of the craft nosed down, dropping the pilot out. A red-and-blue streak drew a parabolic curve under the glider as Superman snatched the falling criminal from his fall.

"Eight seconds."

As he swooped through the sky, the last son of Krypton threw a glance in the direction of a glider hovering over another bank building less than a block away. Banks were thicker in midtown than Cadillacs in Teheran. It was more than a glance that Superman shot at that glider. Its pilot felt unsteady; he looked up and saw his fiberglass kite crackling with intense heat over his head. It was bubbling, becoming disfigured into little globules of molten silicon that could not hold the wind, much less the pilot. As the craft began sailing into the nearest street the pilot made a whirling leap at the bank roof, hoping to land on a particularly padded part of his suit. He didn't land at all.

"Seven seconds."

The flying man carried his two charges by their padded trousers up toward a high ledge of the Galaxy Building and set them down. The ledge was at the level of the building's air conditioning system, so the only way off was by air. On the way down Superman went into a 300-foot power dive at his new targets, his arms flung behind him like the wings of a falcon.

"Six seconds."

He swept between two gliders over two adjacent buildings at a speed just under mach one. The reduced air pressure in his wake dragged the two of them together before they could think. A blast of heat vision Superman tossed back over his shoulder fused the roof doors of the adjoining buildings closed. These two would have nowhere to escape.

"Five seconds."

The lunchtime crowds on the streets hadn't yet figured out what was going on overhead. And an irresistible force came barreling out of the sky at the thronged plaza faster than any eye could possibly follow. He banked toward a scrawny tree standing on the sidewalk in a four-foot round concrete flower pot. Arcing upward, he snatched the plant with him pot and all. By the time he was six stories above the ground he was moving slowly enough so that the pilot of the glider above could see him coming.

"Four seconds."

Seven down out of the dozen. The eighth knew what was coming and couldn't get out of the way. His kite was about to get caught in a tree. Superman pronged his prize like a jouster and continued upward to drop the pilot with the other two on the Galaxy Building ledge.

"Three seconds."

X-ray vision beamed at the earpiece of one pilot filled his head with hellish static. An ultrasonic squeal at the highest D-flat Superman could reach was the right pitch to vibrate another pilot's footrests and handlebars out of his grip. Once the two realized that they were disoriented they would fall to the roofs fifteen feet below them.

"Two seconds."

One of the last two pilots was a few blocks away. He could hear the police loudspeakers playing town crier and feel the diminishing of the vibrations his friends were sending at their assigned bank buildings. He had reached one hand down to a boot holster and was taking aim at the nearest police helicopter.

tchok-tchok-tchok.

Superman caught the three .22 shells in his mouth like jellybeans and spat them out at the three guy lines connecting the pilot to his kite.

ping-ping-ping

The pilot was unconscious on his back.

"One second."

Superman quickly inspected the earphone attachments on the pilots with telescopic and x-ray vision. He had to be sure it was Luthor behind this. He threw his voice, disguised as Luthor's the way it would sound through a radio, at the left ear of the last remaining pilot. "Scrub the mission. Surrender to the police according to our contingency plan," said Luthor's voice.

"Zero."

Swinging over the city for the benefit of those on the ground who were finally catching on to what was taking place, the Man of Steel caught one at a time the three pilots tossed into the air ten seconds ago. They were mercifully unconscious.

And when the police in the four helicopters went to open fire they found, to their surprise, that there wasn't a glider left in the sky. They would collect three suspects from a ledge of the Galaxy Building, three unconscious under a potted tree on the plaza, two in a pile of crashed fiberglass on one roof, and so forth, each armed with a .22-caliber pistol whose firing pin was melted like grilled cheese.

Janet Terry, the new girl in the newsroom, had the presence of mind to get a camera at the window to catch the tail of Superman's performance. Someone always did. By the time Clark Kent walked into the newsroom with a detailed account, the place was a volcano of activity.

Lombard was in the corner of the room with his feet on

the desk smiling as somebody frantically answered the phone and somebody bit a pencil in half as a bulletin came over the newswire and somebody pounded out new copy and somebody demanded that at least one phone line be kept free. Steve had nothing to do until his interview subject showed up.

"Steve, will you talk to me?" Clark asked.

"I'll tell you anything you want to hear."

"What's going on here?"

"Jimmy called up from Princeton and everybody went bazonkas."

"Why? Did you get Superman on film?"

"Sure sure sure. Hey, do you have any idea why he always manages to pick the emergency that's going on near a TV camera?"

"Will you stop it? What did Jimmy say?"

"Well, y'see, it seems there's a big joke on Superman."

"Superman? Joke?"

"Yeah. While Luthor's guys were keeping him busy playing tag the boss was down in Princeton stealing the papers from Albert Einstein's vault. Pretty funny, huh?"

"He what?"

"Stole the papers from Einstein. You don't hear too good, do you, Clarkie?"

9

Oric

Towbee's audience was nearly as heterogeneous as the planet itself—as heterogeneous as his own ancestry. It was the crowd coming out of the temple. The Chief Speaker of the temple was terribly impressed with Towbee's talent, was continually after the minstrel to chant the verses of Sonnabend's prophesies at the services. After a while Towbee finally agreed that his singing at the temple entrance would consist of the verses, along with Towbee's own introductions and transitions. One day of every ten, according to law, had to include attendance at one temple service. That law included anyone who spent more than six consecutive days on Oric, but it did not include Towbee. Towbee was insane.

Among those lingering a moment after the service to listen to Towbee were an arachnoid from Polaris, a tripedal from the Septus Group, even a humanoid all the way from the Central Cluster somewhere. They certainly came a long way these days to get a piece of the action. There must have been sixty of more listeners and no more than two of the same race. And they all very likely thought Towbee was a fool. A mad poet. A singer of silly songs. A diversion from the serious work of slicing up chunks of the Galactic Arm and selling them to the highest bidder. These petty usurers and moneychangers might think more of Towbee if they stopped to notice what he was singing:

It was old when the Guardians had mothers
And Arcturus only glowed in God's eye;
When dominion of the spaceways was another's,
When angels were the only souls to fly.

The prophesy of Sonnabend was tendered,
Bid by Him who did fold the Spiral's tips
For us whom His handiwork has rendered,
To guide us by words of prophet's lips:

When the minions of immortals spread Galactic,
When a thousand cultures dwell in Vega's glow,
When a sailing ship for starflight is a tactic,
When these things all come to pass then we will know

That a hybrid born to Vega has been spreading
Massive strength through an empire built on trade,
And a path to an Arm's rule he is treading;
'Gainst his rule need for freedom sure will fade.

But the heathens would not notice the message, only the medium. They would toss trinkets or treasures into the minstrel's basket according to their station and wealth—this was not payment, actually, but gifts—and they would go back to work.

One of the listeners was listening. The little gray humanoid from the Central Cluster dropped his gift into the minstrel's basket—a modest chip of rare granite—and waited for the rest of the crowd to disperse.

This planet, Oric, was becoming the economic center for this sector of the Galaxy. The world was significantly larger than Earth, but made of lighter material. Its gravity was consequently slightly less strong. No one quite remembered what intelligent race, if any, was native to Oric. The Guardians kept records of such things, but no one else was sufficiently concerned to find out. Three or four thousand years ago by Earth measure of time—which is of dubious value among hundreds of intelligent races whose life spans vary from about twelve years to near immortality—Oric first became a hub of the expanding slave trade in the Galactic Arm. The Arm was that sector of the Galaxy that swung out at the outer tip of the spiral of stars that was the Milky Way. It included all the stars visible to the naked humanoid eye from Earth as well as a few more. It was the last sector to approach the state of civilization.

There was a right and a wrong in the Universe, and that distinction was not very difficult to make.

Slavery, of course, was wrong. This was not to say that there were not certain races or certain individuals among races who were best suited to serve the needs of others. The concepts of right and wrong in the Universe, however, were closely tied with the concept of consistency. Servitude as a commercial commodity is inconsistent, a contradiction in terms. In the practice of buying and selling—or giving and getting, as it was looked at on Oric—a certain freedom of choice is implied on the part of the parties to the transaction. Mandatory servitude does not fit in with that scheme.

No one but scholars in the Ethics of Sonnabend ever went through that thought process when wondering what was right and wrong. Most beings simply knew. The rules were there, had been since Sonnabend laid them down eight billion years ago. The power of the great prophet was such that most of his principles, in some form, found their way into nearly every developed or developing culture in the Galaxy. The principles were not always followed, but they did in fact define very clearly the difference between right and wrong. Loosely translated into English, some of Sonnabend's ethical standards could be stated like this:

Do not bear false witness against your neighbor.

Do unto others as you would have them do unto you.

We are endowed by our Creator with certain inalienable rights including life, liberty, and the pursuit of happiness.

No one had any reliable memory of Sonnabend himself. There was no reliable record left of his exact origins, although there were legends. He so transformed the Galaxy that there was no longer any concept of what the Galaxy was like before him, even among the few who were alive then. That was probably just as well.

It was the voice of the prophet that inspired the founding of the Guardians, a collection of nine immortal humanoid males whose purpose it was to keep order in the Galaxy. That purpose brought them to Oric and the Galactic Arm. The Arm was the last sector of the Galaxy into which the immortals extended their active interest. It was always in their power to come here; there was simply never anything going on here before that demanded their attention. Only wanderers, rogue stars, were outside their jurisdiction.

The Guardians were also inveterate record-keepers. Over eight billion years they recorded the births and deaths of stars as well as the fleeting histories of various forms of life on worlds spinning around those stars. When the star sun Vega was born they watched; when the profusion of black holes provided intelligent beings with power for traveling beyond the speed of light they watched; when Krypton died they watched and they waited.

The little gray humanoid hovered in a corner impassively watching the mulligan stew of bodies zoom this way and that. The minstrel's audience was dispersing, and the grinning, mustachioed, four-armed elf hopped in front of the humanoid. This was Towbee the mad minstrel.

"You're a Malthusian, aren't you, Man?
Of anthropology I'm a fan."

The grinning leprechaun sounded preposterous in any language. The remarkable intentional translators everyone on Oric wore around their necks like amulets decoded the intent of any speaker into the language of the listener, and since Towbee talked in the Orician equivalent of what in English is the entrancing technique called rhyming, so was it translated into whatever was the humanoid's native tongue. The minstrel was always onstage, often jabbering and nonsensical, but always rhythmic.

"I am a native of Malthus," said the impassive face. "You are adept at distinguishing the origins of beings of similar races?"

"A bow in the backbone of fifteen degrees,
A small ball-and-socket joint down in your knees,
Both made my conclusion one of great ease."

Towbee was sounding too intelligent, he thought. It would be a good idea to allay the stranger's suspicions before they had a chance to form. As he spoke he absently caused his instrument—a device capable of making cloudy images from light as well as musical sounds—to form the image of a surface with a round hole. Over the next several minutes an imagined creature of Towbee's own design

65

seemed to try from every conceivable angle to slide his square body into the round hole. The forms Towbee spun were of directed light, not subject to gravitational force, but of apparently infinite mass. They could not be moved or dispersed except by the command of one adept at playing Towbee's instrument. It was simple for the minstrel to feign madness. All he needed to do was appear to open his mind to those around him.

"You've traveled from Galaxy's center to here.
What brings you to Oric, a distance not near?"

"A rumor. I am stopping off on a journey to a star on the rim. A dwarf called Sol. Have you heard of it?"

"I have been there myself, seen remarkable things,
Like a giant world girdled by colorful rings."

"That would be Sol-6, the reason that area is often called the System of the Rings. You are that widely traveled within the Galactic Arm?"

"From Spiral's tip to the shores of sight
I've rode the interstellar night.
So tell me, sir, this rumor queer
That speeds your journey on to there."

"I go to the world Sol-3, called Terra by the beings who inhabit it."

"World of chaos, without plan,
And legendary Superman."

"Yes, the refugee from the destroyed world that orbited Antares. Quite an underachiever, would you say?"

"You've dodged the question, changed our course.
Can Sol-3 hide some great resource?"

The gray being allowed his first faint smile. Towbee could charm the thumbs off a humanoid. "What harm could possibly come of telling one like you? There was a brilliant Terran who died recently and it is said that he left a final mathematical discovery in a secret hideaway designed to open a generation after his death. A generation of Terrans has since passed."

"Terrans contend with rocks and sticks,
With fossil fuels they're in a fix.
How could one of brilliant mind
Be one of those most wretched kind?"

"You have indeed been there, I see. The discoverer was named Einstein and he was in touch with the spirit of Sonnabend. I have heard that he left the secret of trisecting an angle."

"This is an amazing discovery then?
I fear its importance is past my ken."

"I trusted it would be, poet."

For a bit more than a million years the Guardians had been experimenting with a standing corps of agents who acted as a sort of Galactic police force. The Green Lantern Corps consisted of one mortal for each sector of the Galaxy—which was mapped and divided arbitrarily into geographic regions by the Guardians. Green Lanterns were of different races, chosen for their honesty and fearlessness, and were generally romantic, swashbuckling sorts of characters. They were each equipped with uniforms which varied with their respective physiologies and a power battery whose raw energy could be focused through a charm that each carried at all times. Humanoid Green Lanterns wore their charm as a ring.

A Green Lantern was finally appointed to patrol the sector of the Galactic Arm less than four thousand years ago in response to the atrocities perpetrated by the slave trade on Oric. This first Green Lantern of the Arm was a humanoid from the planet that orbited Antares, called Krypton. Not only did he manage to eliminate the slave trade, but he brought the first copies of Sonnabend's chronicles to the Arm and saw to it that a fundamentalist temple was established on Oric. Like the greatest of leaders this Kryptonian Green Lantern joined symbol with substance. The podium for the Chief Speaker of the temple was built out of the auction block from which slaves were sold on that spot. The presence of the temple brought about a following of the prophet Sonnabend that was quite fanatical. Consequently, society on Oric was among the most ritualized in the Galaxy, especially for a society so scrambled with exotic races. It would be necessary, the Guardians knew, for these people to pay a possibly undue lip service to the letter of the Ethics until they truly understood the spirit.

The immortal Guardians were a manipulative breed, and age brought with it subtlety. It was probably no coincidence that the Green Lantern of the sector that included most of the Galactic Arm was a humanoid from Superman's adopted world.

As the man from the center of the Galaxy ambled into the rushing crowd on this planet of great affairs he knew where his poet friend would be going next. The little gray humanoid didn't look an eon over six billion.

10

The Master

Intelligent creatures could not be bought and sold on Oric. Nothing, in fact, could be bought and sold. Gifts were exchanged a great deal—it was the primary occupation of most of the creatures on the planet. It stood to reason, then, that he who had the most possessions, since possessions could only be given and not bought, must be the most beloved by those with whom he comes in contact.

The poet Towbee was ridiculed and had trinkets tossed into his basket. The Master, who held court in a study at the apex of his pyramid-shaped home on Oric, acquired and dispensed worlds with the abandon of a traveling medicine salesman and was the most respected creature on the planet. He was the richest.

The Master lay at a 30-degree angle with his head lower than his feet, four arms hanging below him. His head was directly below the pyramid's apex and the point of light that shone through the open tip. Carlo rolled into the chamber, groveling.

"You may rise up on your wheels, Carlo." The Master's gracious grant of permission to rise was no less a command than the unspoken one that moved Carlo to bow upon his entry. Anyone who entered this room had to swim through an energy that cauterized it, penetrated all within it. There was the conviction that here was greatness. Certainty. Decision.

"Your report, Carlo?" Commands, of course, were quite illegal on Oric, but the Master could hardly help the fact that his requests were strong ones.

"I have cajoled the holder of the last major expanse on the planet Rigel-12 to make a gift of it to you."

"See that he is promised an appropriate gift once our dividend operation has been carried out."

"Yes, Master. Is that all, Master?"

"No, Carlo. Are you aware that a theorist in a nearby predeveloped world has reputedly formulated a solution to the trisection of an angle?"

"Trisection? But that is impossible."

"Obviously it is not. My sources are quite reliable."

"Yes, Master. The simplification of that operation could free up untold time for designers, planners, surveyors."

"I am aware of the implications. I have chosen a plan to send a highly visible messenger to this predeveloped world. His visibility will serve to mitigate against suspicion of his actual purpose. You will prepare for his departure."

"Yes, Master. Is that all, Master?"

"You may leave."

The slave whizzed from the room on command.

11

The Broadcast

Here is the way the show was supposed to start:

At precisely 5:59 P.M. the rerun of whatever the network is rerunning in that time slot goes off and camera 2 in Studio B flashes on Clark Kent. Clark then reads a ten-second "billboard" from the teleprompter—a list of a few top headlines designed to entice viewers of the preceding show to watch the news fifty seconds later.

Here is what happened today instead:

At precisely 5:59 P.M. in the control room adjoining Studio B, Josh Coyle, the director of the news, pressed a button that put the image currently being immortalized by camera 2 over the WGBS-TV air. The teleprompter clearly showed Clark his well-timed 35-word billboard. The red light on the camera which served to alert Clark that he was on the air short-circuited out. So a million viewers across the Metropolis Area of Dominant Influence—a television euphemism referring to the communities a station's signal reaches—were treated to ten seconds of valuable television time during which the inoffensively handsome face of Clark Kent stared blankly out of their picture tubes.

It was not Clark's day.

Somewhere out in space, Clark often thought, there was someone who would receive these television broadcasts that flew off the Earth at the speed of light. Somewhere somebody would figure out that Clark and Superman were the same person. Somebody whose mind was not clouded by human perceptions and prejudices would notice without a touch of effort that two men were one. If that someone was also capable of grasping the idea that no one on Earth knew it, that this was a disguise and a very effective one, that someone would probably catch the irony in Clark's first words today.

"Good evening, this is Clark Kent for WGBS-TV News in Metropolis, on a day when Lex Luthor, the escaped criminal scientist, made a fool out of Superman."

It was times like this when Clark wished he were genuinely schizoid, not just a consummate actor. He had to sit here and challenge his own pride, his masculinity, by all that's holy, in front of over a million people. Could Olivier, Gielgud, Brando, Nicholson pull off this act as effectively? Probably not, Clark thought.

"Luthor turned up today, one week after his disappearance from the maximum security cell block at the Pocantico Correctional Facility, to steal secret documents belonging to the late Dr. Albert Einstein. Jimmy Olsen reports from Princeton, New Jersey."

There was the scene in all its diabolical brilliance. Luthor slipped out the door and through the solid wall as if he'd had super powers all his life. There was the pompous crud flipping back and forth in the sky waving the leather folder and thumbing his nose at the bullets. There he was fading out. And there was Jimmy's verbose, overwritten narration. Jimmy tried hard.

For a long time it was very difficult for Clark to notice when someone was trying hard. Most of what was important to American men in the twentieth century—surviving, prevailing, creating—came easily to Clark. All he ever needed was a good start. He had picked up the English language in a matter of weeks. He seemed to skip right over the single word stage and whole sentences poured from his infant lips. Grammatical rules did not much interest him at first, although his mind was frighteningly sharp. He often came out with statements like, "Me want finish reading *Tale of Two Cities*," and then he did precisely that.

The Kents decided early that at least for awhile they were going to screen his influences very carefully. Martha Kent held, for example, that stories of cutthroats and street urchins of the type Dickens wrote were not the sort of things Clark should be exposed to. She put the *Bible* and lots of Horatio Alger on his reading list. If he were going to insist on reading, she thought, it might as well be decent material. Land sakes, he can wait for *Tom Sawyer* until he's assigned it in school.

By the time Clark Kent was old enough to start the first grade he had been exposed to the wisdom amassed over ten thousand years of human history on Earth. He was even able to extrapolate a bit on that wisdom. He could have discoursed with Descartes and Locke. In an apparent contradiction of his own condition, he held Hobbes and Nietzsche and their ideas of the natural superiority of certain members of society, in contempt. Martha Kent appreciated the influence of her reading list, but she suggested that he substitute simple rejection for the contempt.

The boy was quite aware of the world around him, but he did not yet know who he was. The Kents were careful to ease the knowledge into his mind that he was somehow different. He also knew that this difference was not something to be ashamed of, but it was to be kept secret.

When the time came, his hyperactive mind pondered all the questions his condition posed. There were certain fundamentals, however, that he did not question—axioms at the bottom of his thoughts on any subject that approached his mind: that there was a right and a wrong in the Universe, and that value judgment was not very difficult to make. They were the fundamentals that made Jonathan and Martha Kent who they were and they never seemed inconsistent with anything in Clark's experience.

By the time Clark started school he learned how to wear normal clothes without flexing his muscles through them every time he waved his arm inside a sleeve or took a step in a pair of pants. Jonathan Kent retired as a farmer and started a small business—Kent's General Store on Main Street in Smallville, next door to Sam Cutler's hardware store.

There had been rumors floating around the region about a super-powered tot almost since the day of young Clark's arrival on Earth. At parties, on hayrides, in local newspaper offices and the like people would swear that they had seen a three-year-old boy punch a timber wolf and fly away. Or people would tell about others they knew who told some such story.

With each rash of new super-baby sightings there invariably seemed to follow an outbreak of tales of a were-wolf in some cavern, or a 100-year-old Indian medicine man who hid out in the woods, or the old reliable flying saucers.

The child was the source of a number of unsolved mysteries until the day he revealed himself to the world. There was one point when he flew to London and helped Scotland Yard foil a plot to steal the Crown Jewels. He was the "messiah" once as far as a tribe of Bantu were concerned. He was probably among the most widely traveled children on Earth, even discounting his interstellar journey from a dying world.

When Clark was about ten years old he started wearing glasses and purposely acting timid in front of people other than his parents. That was the Kents' idea; it would allay suspicions that Clark was anything but ordinary.

There was even a girl-next-door romance of sorts in the boy's life. Lana Lang was Clark's age, and she was a sunshiny little red-headed girl. She tended to consider herself a notch or so above the rest of the people in Smallville. Her mother was editor of the local weekly newspaper and her father was a nationally recognized archaeologist who once made the mistake of telling his daughter that the family chose to live in Smallville so that Lana would grow up in a wholesome small town environment. Professor Lang often traveled to New York, London, Metropolis, Rome, as well as the sites of early American Indian excavations. Lana sometimes went with him, and no one in Smallville forgot it when she did.

When he was in his early teens Clark asked his foster mother to design a costume for him—an unforgettable one. He wanted to be recognizable instantly, even to people who had never seen him. The costume would have to be made of the material from the blankets in which baby Kal-El was wrapped when he came from Krypton, as was the indestructible baby jumper he had to wear for most of his first five years. She unravelled the jumper and blankets, Clark cut the material with his heat vision and fused the hems when it was done. He would wear the cape, the skin-tight blue suit and red boots, along with the "S" insignia that would become his symbol.

His foster parents gave him permission to bore a pair of tunnels into the woods outside Smallville. One was connected to the basement of the Kents' home and one underneath the general store. He was going out alone a lot now, stopping fires, scooping people out from under falling trees, tripping up criminals, all from cover or at a speed so fast the eye could not register his presence. Jonathan Kent told him that he was as ready as he would ever be.

A pair of bored, broke adventurers in diving suits tried to rob a bank in Smallville. The event came over a police band radio in the store. Lana was in the store at the time, and Jonathan Kent covered for Clark by asking him to go to the basement and bring up a package from storage. Clark brought back no package. He stripped to the costume he wore under his street clothes, dove through his hidden tunnel and found the robbers jumping into a lake from a pier outside of town. A police car was unable to follow them into the water.

Superboy plopped out of the sky into the lake and threw the pair out as quickly as they fell in. They tried to gun the boy down and he giggled as the bullets bounced harmlessly off his chest. The criminals surrendered in shock and the police were amazed. The patrolmen on the scene took Superboy to Police Chief Parker.

George Parker thought it was a matter for the Mayor's attention. The Mayor thought the Governor should know. The Governor, naturally, used the alien teenager as an excuse to call the President. The President, who was very graceful in strange and bizarre circumstances, promptly invited Superboy to spend the next weekend at the White House.

The last son of Krypton was an instant star. Martha Kent's Horatio Alger books finally seemed to make a little sense.

Smallville was changed but not cowed; the world was cowed. Clark continued to be the timid, studious, dutiful boy helping Pa Kent in the store. Wordly Lana, the girl next door, presumed to develop a crush on the "Boy of Steel," as the out-of-town newspapers called him. Smallville even developed a brief tourist trade, encouraged by a billboard on the water tower and on the entrance roads to the town. It said, "Welcome to Smallville—Home of Superboy."

The Kents were well past child-rearing age when they found that rocket ship near the old farm. On a vacation they both contracted a rare virus over which even their son had no power. They died within a week of each other, Martha Kent first. Jonathan Kent, on the last day of his life and without his wife for the first time in twoscore years, asked his son to stand next to his bed.

Superboy long ago had learned the story of his origin. His power of total recall accounted for most of the story. He was able to fill in most of the blanks by flying at many times the speed of light through space and overtaking the light rays that left Krypton the day it exploded. In this way he actually saw the drama of his infancy reenacted. He knew that he was Kal-El of Krypton, the son of Jor-El, and possibly the finest specimen of humanity in the galaxy. He had broken the time barrier, he could speak every known language on Earth, living and dead. He had been born among the stars and could live among them now if he so chose. He had more knowledge in his mind and more diverse experience to his credit than any Earthman alive could ever aspire to.

Yet he stood at the deathbed of this elderly, generous man whose last Earthly concern was his adopted son's happiness. Superboy listened, because he believed Jonathan Kent to be wiser than he.

Enough of this clowning around in the circus costume, Jonathan Kent told his son. A man is someone who assumes responsibility. To help people in need is right. To grab at every short-lived wisp of glory that tumbles by is wrong.

"No man on Earth has the amazing powers you have," Jonathan Kent told the mightiest creature on the planet. "You can use them to become a powerful force for good.

77

"There are evil men in this world, criminals and outlaws who prey on decent folk. You must fight them in cooperation with the law.

"To fight those criminals best you must hide your true identity. They must never know that Clark Kent is a superman. Remember, because that's what you are, a superman."

And the old man died.

The sale of the business left Clark Kent with enough money to study journalism at Metropolis University, and to pay the taxes on the house in Smallville. Superman could not bear to sell it, so he boarded it up.

People would still call him Superboy for a while. Gradually, though, they would realize that he no longer scooted across the sky giggling as he flew into a hail of bullets. He no longer thought battles of wits with criminals were a fun way to spend the afternoon. Superboy would not be back.

Jimmy Olsen's face on the monitor was fading into the three useable seconds of Superman in action that had been shot through the newsroom window. Clark narrated that, with most of his words heard over the frozen final frame—a remarkable shot of the Man of Steel rolling three unconscious criminals out of his cape to the ground like a sack of rotted pears.

"At the very moment Luthor was pulling off his spectacular robbery, the only person who has ever been consistently capable of thwarting the criminal's plans—Superman—was here. Right outside the Galaxy Building here in Governor's Plaza in Metropolis, stopping what looked to be an attempted multiple bank robbery by twelve men piloting twelve glider-style air vehicles equipped with devices capable of crumbling a vault with sound waves. The robbery attempt bore the unmistakable signature of Luthor himself, and although Superman managed to incapacitate all twelve pilots in ten seconds flat, he was effectively distracted enough so that he could not possibly have gotten wind of the real caper taking place sixty miles away."

Urbane Clark.

Unemotional Clark.

Bland Clark.

He felt like an idiot.

"Jimmy Olsen's next, live from Princeton as Superman tries to pick up Luthor's scent. Also: a little girl noses her way across Long Island Sound, candidates of the Hamiltonian Party sniff the political air, and Mayor Harkness smells a rat in the city budget. After this message."

Puerile writing. Maybe Clark should drop-kick the building into a lunar crater. It was kind of a secret thrill for Clark to watch Superman on the air reenacting the day's triumphs. Having to sit through failures a second time, though, wasn't fun. There was another of those failures coming up.

Coyle the director was in the control booth. "You think we can get it right this time, Clark? We're back on the air in four seconds . . . three . . . two . . . one . . ."

"Less than half an hour after Luthor vanished from the scene, Superman showed up in Princeton. Jimmy Olsen filed this exclusive taped interview."

It was a credit to Clark's acting ability that his face could be replaced on the screen by that of Superman, looking intently at Jimmy Olsen's microphone.

"Superman," Jimmy said on tape, "would you explain to our viewers exactly what it was we just saw you do here?"

"Certainly, Jimmy." That rich voice rippling power and grace filled a million living rooms. "What I was trying to do was reveal a trail of ionized molecules that Luthor's jet boot mechanism should have left behind in the air."

79

At this point Superman and Jimmy's voices were broadcast over the scene Superman was describing, which apparently took place several minutes earlier. Superman was flying to the scene, arriving, motioning everyone in the area outside the Institute building to back away.

"As I arrived and I was backing everyone off the lawn, the reporters and the University people, I was scanning your videotape recorder's imprints to see exactly what happened—where Luthor had been and what he had done. Next I flew off to the nearest large body of water, Carnegie Lake."

On screen, Superman was flying off and almost immediately a long blue cone of swirling liquid appeared over the trees in the direction he'd flown. The cone was half a mile long and followed in the wake of a spinning red-and-blue streak.

"I flew in circles over the lake at super speed to draw up a waterspout and I created artificial air currents around it like a sack so it would follow me through the sky to the Institute here."

The spout was a few hundred feet in the air, directly over the Institute lawn as Superman broke away from it and raced the water to the ground. The tape slowed so viewers could barely catch the sight of the Kryptonian crouching with his back to the camera blowing a massive gust of air from his mouth, creating an updraft as a three-second deluge hit the immediate area.

"The momentary downpour I created," Superman narrated as a swamp clapped the greensward, "was for the purpose of duplicating conditions of a thunderstorm. You may have noticed that I blew upward into the rain as it fell. This is the sort of disturbance that causes electrical charges to clump up in clouds and make lightning bolts."

"You wanted to make artificial lightning where Luthor was? Why?"

"His jet boots had to have jangled up the air he flew

through at least as much as stratospheric winds. This whole area should be loaded with ionic particles of nitrogen."

Darkness and gushes of wet heaves filled the screen, and through it could be seen flashes of sunlight, but no lightning, not even a spark.

"How would that tell you where Luthor went?"

"Well, Jimmy, my theory was that however Luthor escaped, whether invisibly or at super speed, he must have left a trail of ionic particles pointing in his direction. My artificial cloudburst would cause flashes of lightning to point out Luthor's escape route like a beacon."

The fall of water on the tape ended, leaving Superman, soaking wet, standing imposingly against the dew-drenched lawn and the sun. The picture flashed back to Jimmy and Superman speaking minutes later.

"Well, I didn't see any lightning, Superman. Did you?"

"No, actually."

"What are you going to do now?"

"Find Luthor and the Einstein papers."

"But Superman, nobody's been able to turn him up since he escaped. He pulled off this incredible camouflage to keep you away so he could steal this big scientific secret; he figured out some way to get maximum publicity and still cover his tracks completely. You have absolutely nothing to go on, you don't even know what was in the notebook he stole. You're back to where you were when you were just waiting around for him to make the first move. What makes you so sure that you'll be able to find him and bring him to justice now?"

Superman smiled that smile that took over the screen. Redford had a smile like that, so had Eisenhower had, but Clark Kent didn't. "Force of habit," the smile said.

12

The Unveiling

The Zephyrmore Building was rented and maintained by the Coram Management Company, who were retained by Zephyrmore Properties, Inc. Zephyrmore kept the building on a 99-year lease from Barryville Tool and Die Industries, which was a dummy holding company owned by Thunder Corporation. The Chairman of the Board and principal stockholder of Thunder Corporation was a publicity-grabbing, billionaire playboy named Lucius D. Tommytown who did not really exist, never did exist, but was the creation and puppet of Lex Luthor.

Luthor occasionally hired an actor or a disguise artist to portray Tommytown in any of a number of settings: slipping away from an exclusive party, strolling through a European casino tossing hundred-dollar bills at attractive women at the tables, bathing unclothed in a fountain or a public aquarium or a champagne keg. More often, Luthor would spend free moments in jail writing fanciful reports about Tommytown's activities and having them sent to a magazine under the name Brian Wallingford, a well-known freelance reporter also born of Luthor's brow. After each sensational Wallingford story on Tommytown the momentum of the publicity would build and apocryphal sightings and antics of the billionaire would crop up in media all over the world.

Some others of Luthor's made-up people included Chester Horowitz, a prolific inventor, Frank Jones, a habitual contributor to political campaigns, and Faraday Watt, the name on Luthor's United States passport. Luthor owned and operated these imaginary people. He also owned and operated a number of real people, including those in his headquarters in the penthouse of the Zephyrmore Building, as well as the driver of the car in which he was now watching the *WGBS Evening News*.

". . . and a spokesman for the FBI says the bureau expects Luthor's arrest within the next twenty-four hours." Luthor switched off Clark Kent and pushed the stand holding his five-inch television under the dashboard as the car rolled into the building's underground garage.

"Switch on the private radio band, MacDuff."

"Yes, Mr. Luthor." MacDuff's real name was Matthew Jahrsdoerfer, but no one noticed.

"Hello, penthouse?"

"Receiving," said the female voice from the speaker under the dashboard, "clear as a dinner bell."

"This is Poppa Bear," said Luthor. "Care to answer me one question?"

"Shoot, Poppa Bear?"

"Why is the scrambler turned off? You want a police raid up there?"

"Sorry." There was a click over the speaker, followed by storms of static that continued as they talked.

"Every law office in the world has my voice print on file. Don't trip up like that again."

"What?"

"I said that if you want to ruin a good thing, just keep making mistakes like that."

Just static from the other end this time.

"What'd you say?" Luthor asked.

Something about congratulations.

"The car's on the way up the winch."

"What?"

The car, with two honks in the underground garage, opened a wall into a ten-by-ten-foot platform under an open shaft that reached to the roof of the building. The car was on the platform and it was rising.

"Have a hacksaw and a small soldering gun ready when I get up there," Luthor said in the rising car.

"What?"

"A hacksaw."

"Lockjaw?"

"And a soldering iron, dammit!"

Static. The platform stabilized at the penthouse level.

"Listen. Can't you people understand simple English?"

"Did you want something, Poppa Bear?"

Luthor placed the palm and five fingers of his right hand over a panel next to the door which, in response, swung open. He carried the leaden case from the vault into the apartment with him.

"A hacksaw and a soldering iron, you turds. Turn that radio off, the noise makes me feel like I fell asleep in front of the tube waiting for *Sermonette*."

The boss steamrolled into his throne room. The straw-haired woman in her thirties at a desk in a corner put down her shortwave microphone and swung her chair around to face him. Three bright young men in lab smocks stopped conferring over some point on a computer print-out. A middle-aged man at a switchboard cleared all his lines and looked anticipatorily at the entrance. A large high-browed, flat-nosed man and a stunning teenage Vietnamese girl emerged in karate gear from an adjoining mat-

84

lined room to stand and watch. A young red-bearded character looked up from a microscope and removed his glasses. A tall, thin, dark-haired girl in her twenties who was repairing the mechanism of an electronic boom chair in the center of the room froze, looked up, riffled through her box of tools, and scurried up to the imposing figure at the door with a hacksaw and a small soldering gun.

"Thank you, Joanne," he said. "You can go on with whatever you're doing now, I'll let you know when it's time."

They all went back to their particular enterprises. Luthor was in his heaven, all was right with the world.

In another place, under different circumstances, this man might have been a Caesar, a Napoleon, a Hitler, or an Archimedes, a Michelangelo, a da Vinci. A Gautama, a Hammurabi, a Gandhi. But in this place, at this time, he was more. Superman made him more.

As an artist saw objects as an amalgam of shapes, as a writer looked upon life as a series of incidents from which plots and characters could be constructed, Lex Luthor's mind divided the Universe into a finite number of mathematical units. The Earth was four billion people, a day was 86,400 seconds, the Zephyrmore Building was from 16,400 square feet in the penthouse to 62,500 in the lobby and in the first twenty stories. The time he had spent in jail so far this year was three months of thirty days each, three weeks, six days, two hours, and sixteen minutes. This included four weeks, one day, and three hours in solitary confinement during which time he could do nothing more useful than count seconds and scrupulously retain his sanity.

There were other super-criminal geniuses in the world; he had met some of them, dealt with them on occasion. They were chairmen of great corporations, grand masters of martial arts disciplines, heads of departments in executive branches of governments, princes, presidents, prelates, and a saint or two. Unlike Luthor, these men and women chose to retain their respectability. They had trouble coping with honesty.

Luthor was not motivated by a desire for money, or power, or beautiful women, or even freedom. In solitary Luthor decided that his motivation was beyond even the love or hate or whatever it was he had for humanity. It was a consuming desire for godhood, fired by the unreasonable conviction that such a thing was somehow possible. He began by being an honest man. He was a criminal and said so.

He sat down next to the woman at the desk, Barbara Tolley, his clerical assistant. She insisted on being called "B. J." even though her middle name was Arabella.

"Anything pressing?" Luthor asked her as he poured them both a cup of coffee from a beaker rigged to a device that kept it constantly filled with exactly sixteen ounces.

"That gadget you dreamed up in the fall—y'know, the way of making pictures jump off the page like you're wearing 3-D glasses?"

"What about it?" It was a method devised by Luthor's inventor alias, Chet Horowitz, to make holographic images possible on a flat surface so that a picture would appear to hang several inches off a page.

"Every major paperback company in town made a bid for the process. It seems there's this whole new group of people whose job it is to package books like detergents or political candidates or something."

"And they want to put this thing on paperback covers. Good idea. You walk down an aisle looking for a cookbook, and the one that catches your eye has a cover with lobster thermidor hanging into the aisle. So what's the problem?"

"Chet Horowitz stands to make a small fortune on it."

"Yes?"

"He made a small fortune on the gizmo that keeps electric plugs from shocking babies, and another small fortune on the new riveting gun. That's three small fortunes since January. Bernie the accountant says you're overspending and we won't have enough to pay Chet's income taxes this year."

Luthor smiled.

"All right, genius." B.J. gave him the indulgent look she kept as a defense against his. "If the solution's so damn obvious why didn't Bernie think of it himself?"

Luthor obviously had B.J. by the intrigue glands. This happened so seldom that he sat silently long enough to see her eyes crinkle. Then he solved the accountant's problem: "We don't have to pay Chet Horowitz' income tax at all this year. Let a process server try to find him. We're criminals, remember?"

"Right." B.J. uncrinkled herself and squeezed the bridge between her eyes. "But why do you have to persist in making the rest of us feel so inadequate?"

"That's how I stay in charge, lady-pal. Napoleon did it with conquest, Supes does it with pretension, my mother did it with guilt. I manage with brute competence."

Luthor reminded himself of a song he'd once written which had a line that went: "To live outside the law you must be honest." He'd slipped the lyrics to a young singer he met in a bar in Minnesota. The guy had a lousy voice and Luthor felt sorry for him at the time. When he heard the line again he didn't recognize the song that surrounded it. He resolved, from then on, to be his own editor.

B.J. was on the verge of making small talk. Bad habit of hers. Luthor decided it was party time, so he hopped to his feet.

"Your attention, please!" he addressed his employees. There was immediate silence. "Would everyone please follow me into the Meditation Room?"

Luthor led a procession to the penthouse balcony where

his fingerprints unlocked the door to a big room whose walls were completely covered with bright green drapes. He held the lead case under his arm like a minister's prayerbook as they filed in, all but one wearing intensely solemn expressions. Luthor sat in the room's sole piece of furniture, a swiveling stool.

"I have obtained," Luthor continued, careful not to look at B.J.'s smirk, "the last vestige of the life of a great man. The single thing from his life that he chose to leave for posterity after his death. If you will pay attention . . ."

Luthor turned to the curtained wall, placed the chair facing it, and put the case and the tools down in front of the chair. He walked to the corner and pulled the curtains' drawstring. They peeled away to reveal, larger than life, a magnificent portrait in acrylics of Albert Einstein. Luthor ignored his band of disciples and now spoke directly to the portrait.

"You see? I brought it, like I said I would. We couldn't let it fall into the hands of someone who couldn't appreciate it, right?" He was as sincere as an eight-year-old child talking to a gnarled tree. "Here, I'll show you."

Luthor held the lead case between his legs, huffing as he sliced off a corner with the saw. The others in the room looked on silently, afraid to change expressions because they only partially understood, as he painstaking softened a piece of the casing next to the opening with the soldering gun, then ripped it open further. Piece by piece, inch by inch, until two sides of the casing were disconnected and the corner could be folded down. Inside was a thin brown folder holding just a few pages.

Luthor looked at the cover of the folder and furrowed his brow at the neatly typed message on the card glued to the front. He opened the folder, blinked, and winced at what he saw.

"Gibberish. What is this nonsense? Code? This isn't

English. Isn't German. What the devil's clawed hooves is this?"

B.J. flew into the vacuum Luthor's equanimity left behind. "What's wrong, Lex? What is it?"

"Look. Look at this. He must've gone nuts. He spent twenty years looking for a Unified Field Theory and it made him crackers. What is this chicken vomit?"

"It's writing. Calm down, Lex. Get out of here. Everybody out of here. End of the party. Back to work." The audience all shuffled out, not daring to murmur, and the woman closed the door behind them.

"It's not writing. It's not Latin, not Greek, not Arabic. Never saw a code like that. What is it? What is it?"

She understood that he was used to solving problems. As a child his response to adversity was a tantrum. As an adult he revelled in the fact that he was outside the law. In his mind the totality of the Universe was as real as the drugstore down the block. When everything comes that easily, a setback is a trauma. All she had to do was hold him down until he started coming back of his own accord. He was almost around.

"Code?" he asked.

"Yes. Or another language. A lost one, maybe."

"That code-breaker. The one I got the job for at the CIA. You know the one. Get him up here. Blindfolded. Right away. And the crooked philologist, the one serving the six-year term for trying to put a wiretap on the Kremlin hot line. Look over the jailbreak file and find one that'll work for him."

"All right. What'll you do, Lex?"

"You'd better leave me alone awhile." Luthor walked over to the portrait on the wall. "I've got to have a talk with the professor."

13

The Entertainer

A world whose most public figure is a super-powered alien from a lost planet is not startled or horrified or even particularly curious at the visit of an eccentric, erratic character from somewhere in space. The world is amused.

Towbee visited Earth briefly a few years ago and caused some trouble for a day or so. Apparently this character was a minstrel of some sort, like the wandering troubadours who turned up in feudal courts, only Towbee traveled among the outposts of space entertaining the idle, the harried, the lonely. He sang, he clowned, he cast images with an instrument that formed clouds of air into corporeal shapes as well as made music. When he came to Earth, he said, it was because he was in a creative slump and he was running out of stories to tell.

He'd heard stories about Superman and wanted to see whether he was real. One day a repulsive flying lizard swooped down from the sky over Metropolis, snatched up Clark Kent in its claws, and dramatically dangled the hapless fellow over the city. Towbee would see what Superman would do and then go on his way with a story of the remarkable Kryptonian to add to his repertoire.

The minstrel hovered twenty-two thousand miles above the city in his one-man flying toychest for several minutes before he caught onto the fact that while Superman wore civilian clothes he pretended not to have his powers. This was a cultural idiosyncrasy, Towbee thought, which to understand would require more study of Earth's society than Towbee cared to undertake. The storyteller quickly fashioned a stand-in Clark Kent. The real Clark Kent immediately ducked into a real cloud, became Superman, and disposed of the illusion menace in characteristically flamboyant fashion. The Man of Steel found the source of all the trouble and gave Towbee a threatening lecture on social responsibility. Towbee happily left the Solar System and wrote his own equivalent of an epic poem about the incident.

Anything for his art.

This latest trip to Superman's city, Towbee decided, would be worthy of Earth's greatest showmen. Ringling Brothers' Barnum and Bailey Circus was in Metropolis at the time. The circus was managed by a young animal trainer named Gunter Gabel Williams who entered the center ring standing on the back of a galloping elephant and holding a leashed leopard.

At ten-thirty A.M. two days after the theft of the Einstein document all vehicular traffic in midtown Metropolis came to a honking halt. Necks craned and jaws dropped and heads hung out of windows as the zany four-armed singer from space materialized on Fifth Avenue.

Pulled by a herd of seven Indian elephants each in a different color of the rainbow was a 90-foot-long transparent fishtank. The tank was filled with water which in turn was filled with a great blue whale floating calmly on the surface. On the whale's back was Towbee rocking in

91

an easy chair with his feet up on the edge of a tub in which a large baboon was bathing. With one pair of hands Towbee played a melody on his instrument as he sang "Annie Laurie," and with the other pair he held a copy of the previous day's *Daily Planet* and read. And curled up under his legs was a Siberian tiger, sleeping like a fallen redwood.

Police cordoned the entrances to Fifth Avenue. Thousands of people followed the procession past Governor's Plaza toward the park. Towbee and his bizarre litter passed within sight of the offices of all the city's television stations and by the time he rolled a block the swarm of newsmen and police who were following him were in danger of being trampled by the calm elephants as they mechanically pulled their load.

The alien wailed "Annie Laurie" gradually louder and louder. When he was finally loud enough so that his voice drowned even the din of midtown, the elephants and the aquarium ceased their progress up the street, and the grand marshal rose from his seat to address the world from the back of his whale.

Towbee's instrument fashioned other-worldly sounds into a haunting, buoyant melody, and he and his pets and the faces and minds of everyone who saw him were clouded with remarkable shapes and colors in an ineffable random pattern as he sang:

A clown has come
A splash of rum
I'll make you grin
Halibut's fin
And send your tears
Out of your day
Apples and pears
Hurrah and hooray
With shape and sound

Cashews by the pound
And colors flying
Laundry drying
Dreams and streams
A clock you wind
Gleams from themes
An organ grind
You'll surely leave your mind behind

And in a swirl and a splash of colorful clouds Towbee leaped from the back of his whale, defying gravity to float to the ground. As the whale and its tank, the water, the tub, the baboon and the sleeping tiger and the seven elephants of seven different colors melted into a three-dimensional kaleidoscope that dispersed like smoke. Towbee, this street dream's creator, bowed low in all directions to the cheers of the breathless crowds.

Towbee motioned with his four hands for his audience, including the reporters, to draw closer as he explained himself. (*"I've brought myself to this, your Earth/To give a new career its birth."*) He explained that this world was in a very exciting stage of its civilization, one in which art and technology were intersecting like parallel lines at infinity. Communication was worldwide and nearly instantaneous, he said, and what people chose to communicate, mostly, was art: songs, plays, performances of all kinds. (*"I've traveled from my homeworld far/In order to become a star."*) The self-proclaimed clown intended, he said, to see the city's most successful starmaker and ask for a recording contract.

A reporter asked for another sample of Towbee's work and the alien obliged:

Good Sonnabend did talk of days far distant,
Of wonders which have lately come to be
And births and trends historic now existent
This prophecy was handed down to me:

When the minions of immortals spread Galactic,
When a thousand cultures dwell in Vega's glow,
When a sailing ship for starflight is a tactic,
When these things all come to pass then we will know.

Easily ten thousand people stood in Fifth Avenue,
entranced. It was in front of the old aluminum-spired Radio Corporation Building.

On the rounded tip of the spire, unnoticed over the
crowd sixty-five stories below, sat the last son of Krypton,
who wondered.

That a hybrid born to Vega has been spreading
Massive strength through an empire built on trade . . .

14

The Crooked
Philologist

Luthor sat in his private study, poring over the document with Elvin Lovecraft, the Central Intelligence Agency's code expert.

"Got anything yet?" Luthor was testy.

"No," Lovecraft said, "but it kind of reminds me of a code British Naval Intelligence once used. I cracked that."

"Aren't the British on our side?"

"Sure they're on our side."

"Then what were you doing cracking their spy code?"

"What do you think? They send us bulletins about their state secrets? They're like everyone else. This code, see, it was based on the brand names of Moroccan coffee manufacturers."

"Come again?"

"Coffee manufacturers. There are twenty-six companies listed with the Moroccan government as licensed to distribute coffee, one for each letter of the Italian alphabet."

"Why Italian?"

"Italian was picked at random, also because the Italians are preoccupied enough with their own instability. They wouldn't be interested in the affairs of the British government."

"What happened with the coffee companies?"

"Oh. Well, they looked up each coffee company in the Moroccan financial journal and got the first word in the name of the company three listings below the coffee companies. These were listed in reverse alphabetical order and each stood for one letter of the alphabet."

"The whole word stood for a letter?"

"Yeah. Really unwieldy. Like the word 'and' came out spelled 'texture-consolidated-general' or whatever its equivalent was in Moroccan and Italian."

"And this code from Einstein reminds you of that?"

"Yeah."

"How so?"

"That one was impossible to crack, too."

The code expert turned back to the document and his notes, huffing and snorting and crossing things out. Luthor stared at him trying to decide whether to feel amazed, confused, or disgusted. He couldn't make up his mind, so he went into the next room to watch a videotape of the news that B.J. prepared for him every day.

The thirty-sixth floor of the Galaxy Building was bleached white with tiling on the floors, porous ceilings that ate sound, glass doors, and marble wall paneling broken only by carefully selected prints of abstract paintings with stainless steel frames. Jan Schlesinger perched in the chair behind the reception desk, pleasant but not friendly, attractive but not sexy. The last girl to sit behind that desk was dismissed when she came to work one day wearing Argyle socks.

With a swirling spout of earth-colored clouds formed in front of Jan and then consolidated into the form of a grinning, four-armed man about five feet tall she was sure she was being tested.

"May I help you, sir?"

"My purposes I will not hedge,
I've come to speak with Morgan Edge."

"Yes, sir. Do you have an appointment?"

"Just tell this Edge that Towbee's here
And he will see me, never fear."

Mr. Edge is only available by appointment, sir. Galaxy Communications is a very large company. If you would write a letter specifying what you would like to talk to Mr. Edge about, I'm sure it would be a better idea."

"T-O-W-B-double-E.
Tell him that and he'll see me."

"Towbee?"
"That's my name. The very same."

"Just a moment, sir." Jan pressed a button on her desk's interoffice picturephone and addressed the facelift that flashed on the screen. "A Mr. Towbee here, he says he's sure Mr. Edge will want to see him."

"Towbee?" the facelift said. "Did you say Towbee?"

"Yes, uh, T-O-W-B double-E."

"Does he have four arms and a mustache and speak in rhymes?"

This has got to be a test, Jan thought. Keep your cool, girl. "Yes, he does," Jan said.

"Stand by a second." The screen flashed a test pattern, Jan heard shuffling and some sort of clanking down the hall, and she smiled at the minstrel's pleasantly grotesque face.

The test pattern was replaced by the facelift with a smile clamped to her cheeks. "Jan, please direct Mr. Towbee to Mr. Edge's office."

She told Towbee to turn left at the corner and go through the door at the far end of the corridor. He followed her directions, and she allowed herself a wide grin while no one was looking. Her job was secure.

The five-minute news summary that originated sixteen floors below Jan three hours earlier at 11 A.M. was videotaped in Luthor's penthouse, and now he was watching it. B.J. sat behind the television as he watched, reading from a red file folder.

Jimmy Olsen was on the screen saying, "You may remember that Towbee was the name of an alien who loosed an apparently harmless flying lizard on Metropolis some years ago. The only one who actually met that Towbee at the time was Superman, and there has been no word from him as to whether that alien and the space minstrel who appeared in the city today are one and the same. But here is what the minstrel had to say today."

"Underground with the diesel mole?" B.J. asked.

"No," Luthor answered. "He's on an upper level."

"Shatter the wall with a sonar gun?"

"No, too spectacular."

"Disguise him as a guard?"

"Needs too much planning."

Towbee was on the screen now, singing, "And a path to arm's rule he is treading . . ."

"Smuggle in jet boots?" B.J. asked.

"He's not athletic enough."

"Hotdogging with the helicopter?"

Luthor thought a second. "Simple, direct, not something I would be immediately suspected of, maybe. Yes. Who's the best pilot not serving time?"

"MacDuff."

"Give him a schematic of the prison and send him in here for his working orders," Luthor said as Towbee was replaced on the screen by the face of Jimmy Olsen, "and rewind that tape. I want to hear what that spaceman said again. The part about a prophesy or something."

Edge was close to fifty, everyone knew, but no one would have guessed that. He smiled a lot, the way a cobra smiles. A few strands of gray salted his brown hair. He affected a holder with a cigarette, which he occasionally lit. He was quite experienced at dealing with potential recording stars, and he considered the fact that this one was alien to the planet an afterthought.

"Quite a show you put on today, Mr. Towbee."

"The show's not the important part,
I need a stage to make my art."

"Of course. And you feel the recording division of Galaxy is the proper forum for that art."

"To Galaxy I'd make a gift
Of songs and tales your souls to lift."

98

"A gift. Of course." He wasn't so different from artists and creators Edge already knew. Talking about bestowing their vision upon the world like a gift from Heaven. In the halls of this building Towbee and his kind were just talent. Not talented people, just talent, a commodity. Talent had a market value based on demand, like eggs or cars or information or any of the other commodities in which merchants dealt.

"Just show me to a microphone,
I'll sing and show you worlds unknown."

"Yes. Well, I'm afraid you will have to work out the particulars with Clete Mavis, the president of our recording division. He's on the West Coast right now, but I will direct him to work out a deal with you as to—"

"You speak to me of deals, good man?
Vulgarity not my plan."

The preposterous little creature was offended. He was standing up, ready to leave, when Edge's business sense piped up with, "That's just an expression we use. A euphemism. Deal. Like in a card game." Edge wasn't sure of what he meant by that, but Towbee seemed to like it.

Towbee sat down again and told the executive that he was relieved. He had one request to make of Edge, however. He wanted to know where he could find back issues of the *Daily Planet*. Edge asked a secretary to take Towbee to the records room on the sixth floor.

Towbee pored over copies of the *Planet* printed in the past several days. He picked up a copy from two days ago that had a large picture of Lex Luthor on the front page. He stared at it intensely for several seconds, turned into a puff of smoke and vanished.

Luthor gave MacDuff his instructions a few minutes before three in the afternoon. On Clark Kent's broadcast three hours later, following the lead story on Towbee, there was an account of a spectacular escape from the Pocantico State Correctional Facility. A helicopter touched down in the prison courtyard and an obscure little man named John Lightfoot scurried in to take off before some of the guards could even turn their heads and see. The armored hull of the copter pinged with bouncing bullets as it sped upward at a 60-degree angle, possibly toward a mother craft, maybe a jet circling above, before prison hardware could be brought into play against it. The escape was daring, apparently flawless, and nearly successful.

While the copter was still within sight of the prison grounds, it began to weave in the air. It coughed, sputtered, and lost altitude. It crashed in a wooded area less than a mile from the Pocantico facility. In the wreckage were two bodies, charred beyond belief. Lightfoot was a professor of linguistics who was once unfortunate enough to become involved in a scheme with a collection of incompetent industrial spies. In less than a month he would have been eligible for an almost sure parole. No one understood how he could have known anyone who would attempt such an escape, or why the linguist would agree to a dangerous adventure this late in his sentence.

Some prison guards who saw the crash claimed to have seen a kind of swirling colorful mass envelop the helicopter before it went out of control. This was obviously an illusion caused by the distance.

"Damn!" Luthor told the television. B.J. realized that if he had a choice between talking to a mechanical object or another person in a room Luthor would invariably address the object. "Is that birdseed brain still working in the study?" This was a non-rhetorical question, which meant Luthor was talking to her.

"He hasn't come out. Last time I was in there, he hadn't made any progress."

"Cretin hasn't even decided whether it's a code or some kind of foreign language. Now that Lightfoot's gone, we're stuck with—whuzzat?" Someone below the penthouse was banging on the floor.

"Somebody's banging on the floor," B.J. observed.

"Very good. Tomorrow we try potty training. Tell me something."

"What?" He banged again.

"Has anyone new moved in downstairs?"

"No." And again.

"Is anyone in this penthouse dancing or moving furniture or doing anything that would annoy someone downstairs?"

"No." The banging was constant now.

"Have we ever in the past had downstairs neighbors who bang on our floor just to be cranky?"

"No."

"Then why the flying moose ears don't you send somebody downstairs to see what somebody's trying to tell us?"

Six minutes later Luthor was presented with the smiling figure of John Lightfoot, linguist extraordinaire, wearing a coat over ragged prison fatigues and slicing his face with a smile.

"Explanation?" Luthor said crisply.

"I made it out of the helicopter in time and landed in a tree. It was horrible."

"MacDuff?"

"The pilot? He's gone, poor boy."

"The news reported two charred bodies."

"Did they? Well, I don't suppose they want to admit the loss of a prisoner. The authorities like the public to believe in poetic justice, you may have noticed."

"Very smooth, fella. You haven't told me yet how you managed to find me. Let's hear it."

"Where else was I to go? I hitched a ride with some young people and—"

"Hang the ride. How'd you find my headquarters?"

"Oh, that. *Pygmalion.*"

" 'Scuse me?"

"*Pygmalion. My Fair Lady.* It was the reason I became interested in philology. I read George Bernard Shaw's *Pygmalion* when I was a boy and was impressed with the man who was able to tell where people live by their regional accents. I always wanted to be able to do that."

It was the sort of contrived story that so fascinated Luthor he had to accept it. "You compared the idiosyncrasies of my speech with those of other people on my staff, and you determined what part of the city we frequent. Brilliant."

"Yes. So I came here and saw only three buildings in the area that had penthouses. The pilot, rest his soul, had time to mention we were going to a penthouse. I counted fifty-three floors from the outside of the Zephyrmore Building, but only fifty-two were listed on the elevator. I hope you didn't think me too bold when I knocked on your floor."

Maybe Luthor had underestimated the mousy little man he'd met in prison. Maybe, dare he hope, there would be someone around here intelligent enough to hold a coherent conversation. "Not too bold at all, Lightfoot. Shall we go to work?"

"Fine idea."

15

The Caper

Luthor gave the Lovecraft clown his three-hundred-dollar daily consultation fee and had him blindfolded and deposited outside his Alexandria, Virginia, home. Lightfoot seemed to know what he was doing.

"It's quite fascinating," Dr. Lightfoot told Luthor once the linguist had the chance to study the Einstein document for a few minutes. "This is obviously not only a foreign language, but an altogether new language form. Look, there are no prepositions."

Luthor did not quite know why that was significant, but Lightfoot seemed impressed.

"And the conjunctions," Lightfoot said, his eyes wide, "at least I think they're the conjunctions. They seem to be tacked onto the subjects of clauses like prefixes."

So Luthor was impressed.

"Lord! This is fascinating!" Lightfoot marveled.

Luthor was secure for the first time since he tore open the great prize in his meditation room. Lightfoot was the best there was at the science of languages. In days, maybe a week or two, Lightfoot would be able to give Luthor some idea of what treasure of knowledge it was that Einstein saw fit to preserve for the generation that followed his own.

About an hour into Lightfoot's study he began pacing around the room and stopped making comments to Luthor at all. He would stand up, walk a few steps, occasionally bump into a chair or a priceless antique clock or a wall without noticing, then scurry back to the desk to scribble something in a notebook. Luthor decided it was time to leave him alone.

As usual, the main hall of the penthouse was swarming with little groups of extremely competent specialists in different areas who had sold their respectability for creative freedom and lots of money. Luthor corrected a minor error in a calculation done by two young computer-data analysts. He looked over a hydraulic missile-launching ramp on the balcony that his crack mechanic was trying to repair and pointed out the problem to her. He was showing an employee who was a retired chemistry professor from Amherst how to produce Argon Tetrafluoride without combustion when the study door flew open.

Luthor had no friends, really. He had a few cronies, a lot of employees and one enemy. He also had a few marks. One of his major talents was the ability to turn potential enemies, generally people who had something he wanted, into marks. Even Superman was a mark once, or was he a friend? People called him Superboy then, even though he was the same guy. When Luthor remembered anything that far back he usually made a point of doing so for the purpose of accumulating some anger in his system. Anger clouds the truth as surely as does love, terror, or grief.

The Jefferson-Baker Science Contest was an annual competition that a large industrial corporation initiated when Lex Luthor was in grade school. Around that time, there was a good deal of fear in the American Corporate Empire that the nation's educational system was not capable of producing enough bright and creative scientists to maintain the country's technological preeminence over the coming generation. The people who owned and directed the Jefferson-Baker Corporation thought that it would be a good idea to allocate a certain amount of money each year for scholarships to the high school students who could, with limited resources and no adult assistance, produce the most original and ingenious new scientific or mechanical devices.

Lex also thought that this was a good idea, and he realized that while the Jefferson-Baker Science Contest was never likely to single out the next Einstein or Edison, or even the next Peter Goldmark, it was a fine way to strengthen the resolve of those remarkably talented young people who, through chance or politics or the mood of the judges, were not winners of scholarships. Young Lex Luthor, however, felt that his own resolve was already sufficiently strong to achieve greatness, and that he did not need to lose the contest. It would be nice, however, if he could pay his way through a university or technological institution of a stature he considered acceptable. Pop wasn't going to cough up the tuition, even if he could afford it. Lex would have to do it himself. The top Jefferson-Baker prize of ten thousand dollars would about cover it.

Lex decided that he could minimize his chances of losing by first considering (1) what sorts of projects had won in the past and (2) who this year's judges were likely to be and what they were probably interested in.

After careful consideration he decided that (1) the projects that tended to win the big prize were generally flashy, usually expanded on a current popular fad in the scientific community and were easy to explain to the public in magazines or on television, and (2) the panel of judges seemed to be weighted, from year to year, in the direction of scientific technicians—rather than theorists—who were more likely to be impressed with a clever demonstration of an old principle than with a wholly new idea. All right, Lex thought, if what they wanted was showmanship he would blow them all away.

In November of the year Lex Luthor was in the ninth grade, three boys from his class showed up in the Waterville Valley High School gymnasium for the state eliminations in the Jefferson-Baker Science Contest. Out of a spinning silk ribbon and a copper toilet tank float, Pete Ross built a Van de Graaf electrostatic generator which could shoot tiny bolts of lightning at a flower box and, theoretically, stimulate the growth of plants. Clark Kent showed off a crude, nearly indescribable harness-and-pulley system which, Clark said, simulated for prospective space travelers the condition of low gravitation. A person in the harness would hang parallel to the ground, walk/swinging along a wall like a pendulum, and feel as though he or she were hopping high off the ground/wall with each step. Lex's exhibit consisted of an empty platform with a sign off to one side that said, simply, "MAGIC."

Students spent the morning setting up their projects, testing them out, standing back to admire the way they looked, checking out the competition to make sure no one had a better idea. Pete Ross, typical of the entrants in the room in that he was reasonably sure that he would win or that he ought to, asked Clark Kent if he had seen Lex yet.

"I gave him a ride over here in my Pa's pickup," Clark said. Clark had a special daylight driving license that allowed him to drive farm vehicles earlier than he would normally have been. Jonathan Kent had only recently sold his farm and the license had not yet expired.

"Then he got here the same time you did? It's nearly one o'clock. What's he been doing?"

"I don't know. The judges are supposed to come around at two."

"Yeah. Every time I asked him what he's doing he wouldn't even tell me if he was entering the contest for sure. What'd he bring? Anything?"

"Just a big steamer trunk. I had to help him carry it. Last I saw he was dragging it through that door behind his platform."

"Really? You saw it?" Pete's apprehension was oozing up through his cool. "Did you see what he had in it?"

"Yeah. He opened it once when I went to set up my harness."

"What'd he do? What was in it? What'd you see?"

"That sign over there."

"Just the sign? Nothing else?"

"Yeah. See? It says 'Magic.' "

"I can read."

For awhile, nobody but Pete Ross and Clark Kent appeared to notice the empty platform among the eighty-two other exhibits that the entrants stuffed into the room. People walked by it, around it, generally ignored it. At about half past two the mother of one of the entrants walked over the platform, hopped into the air, spun around and shrieked.

"How dare—uhh," the woman looked behind her and down at the floor. "I thought there was somebody there. I saw him. He crouched behind me."

People's heads turned, a few smiled. The people nearest the woman shuffled nervously. One man, evidently her husband, told her in a low voice that there was no one there and that she should calm down.

"I saw him. I really saw him, plain as life. I think I saw him, a boy with curly brown hair. He must have run off into—no, I suppose he didn't."

Just then the woman's husband yelped. Lex Luthor was

standing deferentially at the closed door behind the platform. No one had seen him come through the door. No one but the man who yelped had been looking.

"I wonder if I could have your attention for a moment," Lex announced. As he said this he appeared to step onto the platform and walk to the center of it, oblivious to the man who, with a hand clapped over his mouth, was leading his wife away. For the next several minutes no one in the room paid any attention to anything other than young Lex Luthor because the next thing he did was pull a rabbit out of the air.

"I suppose you want to see me do that again, don't you?" His audience agreed. "Well, it's a cardinal rule of magic," Lex explained, "that no self-respecting magician does the same trick twice in succession, at least not the same way. But then again, no self-respecting magician goes around without a top hat, so—"

Lex reached both hands into the air in front of him and feigned a surprised expression when a silk top hat appeared in his hands out of nowhere. There was, of course, a rabbit in the hat.

"There you go, Pierre," he said as he put the animal on the floor next to its mate, "go play with Marie. Uh-oh, I think you two are getting along too well for a mixed audience. Shoo!" and the pair ran to the edge of the platform, where they again vanished into the air that had apparently spawned them.

For the next fifteen minutes Lex mesmerized the crowd with his snappy patter and his ability to pull out of the air objects of increasing size—a pair of shoes, a full dress suit which he put on, tossing all but his skivvies into nowhere, a magic wand, a large radio, a steamer trunk— and throw them back again to vanish completely.

For his last trick, Lex made a running leap into his audience, and seemed about to land on the head of a startled man when Lex vanished. He floated back onto the stage, as if emerging from a hole in space, wearing his full dress suit and silk hat, riding the bare back of a brown mare. "She looked lonely, so I invited her along."

As the amazed, applauding collection of people watched, a man hollered from the back of the room, "That's Elsa. You no-account little horse thief, what're you doing riding on my Elsa?"

"I'm glad to know her name," the boy laughed as the irate farmer lumbered across the room and onto the platform. "I was hoping her owner would turn up. Adds just the right amount of drama to my finale, don't you think?"

The man had been amused enough by the performance so far, but he was no longer in any mood for theatrics. His grandfather had told him that a horse thief was the lowest form of life on Earth and he believed everything his grandfather told him. His grandfather also told him he was awarded the Medal of Honor in the Civil War, although the old man was born in 1871. The farmer grabbed at his animal's bridle and nearly swallowed his chewing tobacco when his hand passed through it as it nothing were there. He grabbed for the horse's mane, for her neck, for the collar of Lex's jacket as the boy climbed off the animal's back. It was like clutching at a beam of light. It was exactly like clutching at a beam of light.

"Please don't be angry, sir," Lex told the farmer who was now clawing at him, standing in the same space as the boy. "Maybe this is the best way to explain it. You might notice that Elsa and I don't cast shadows right now . . ."

Lex took the horse's bridle and walked to the side of the platform with her, seeming to disappear with her as they walked past a certain point in space. The door in front of which Lex had first appeared now opened from the inside. From behind the doorway Lex led Elsa, whole and healthy.

". . . but now we do. What you have just seen," Lex explained, "was a demonstration of holograms more sophisticated, I believe, than they have ever been constructed before. All of what you just saw were images, projections of what I was doing in a space I set up in a locker room behind that door. The voice that seemed to come from my projection actually came from a speaker I set up behind my 'Magic' sign."

All but one of the six people who were judging the entries—they were all men—smiled their appreciation of the performance. The sixth wore a dubious look. Only one of the judges pretended to understand fully as Lex explained the system that allowed him to project his animate, live image into an adjoining room, and that judge was only pretending. Everyone else in the room except for Clark Kent and the farmer was clearly and completely impressed.

Clark Kent knew about the setup hours earlier and had been impressed then. The farmer, grumbling, led his horse back to her stable a quarter-mile down the road from the high school. The one-thousand-dollar scholarship award for the state's best entry in the Jefferson-Baker Science Contest went that afternoon to Pete Ross.

Lex was despondent. The dubious judge had realized that Lex was from Smallville and assumed that Superboy had helped him with his extraordinary entry in the science contest. It was not true. It was also technically not against the rules, since Superboy was not an adult. On the slim chance that Superboy had not, in fact, helped young Luthor, the judge convinced his fellow judges to give top honors to another boy from Smallville, Pete Ross, who had put together a very impressive project. The idea was for the judges both to be fair and to maintain the integrity of the contest. They did neither.

Lex Luthor was raised on anger. Superboy was raised on responsibility. Superboy knew that it was not logical,

110

but that it was quite proper, for him to feel responsible for Lex's loss of the prize. He was worried that the boy would do something self-destructive. Lex was more likely to blow up Waterville Valley. Superboy determined to soften the disappointment.

The day after the contest, Superboy asked a Smallville alderman, Jonathan Kent, for a special building permit for a temporary structure on an acre of village property at the edge of town. The Mayor was scheming with the Board of Aldermen—unsuccessfully, as it would turn out—to make Superboy a paid public relations agent for Smallville, and the Board thought that this permit would be a good first step toward that end.

Superboy got his permit a week later at a regular Board of Aldermen meeting. Within half-an-hour after the Mayor signed the permit there was a white and red, flat-roofed, one-story, forty-by-twenty-foot building on the lot. Superboy equipped the building with rare chemicals and minerals, deep freeze, compression chamber, centrifuge, an electrical generator fueled by the heat from a pocket of natural gas that lay seven hundred feet below Smallville, and every other useful gadget he could think of. Superboy set Lex Luthor down at the new laboratory's front door and wished him luck.

The way Luthor now remembered it, his entry in the rinky-dink science contest and his faking of disappointment afterward were simply an elaborate scheme to get Superboy to build him a lab. Some weeks afterward, young Lex Luthor received two registered letters. One was from the Westinghouse Corporation, asking him to work for them the following summer, using their resources, helping to develop the new science of holography. The other was from the Criminal Court of Waterville Valley informing him that charges of horse thievery had been brought against him, and that his trial was scheduled for the beginning of the summer. By the summer, Lex

Luthor would have more important things to worry about. The development of holography was set back at least a generation.

The study door in the penthouse flew open and Dr. John Lightfoot tromped out of the room, down the four steps into the main hall, and walked across the room mumbling and looking down and scratching under his left ear all the time. He bounced off the glass door to the balcony, walked in two tight circles, and ran back to the study when his face lit up.

A minute later Lightfoot called out, "Air! I need some air!"

Like a photon out of quasar Luthor was at the study, where he slammed into the little philologist who was absently wandering through the doorway. As the two helped each other up the thought briefly skipped through Luthor's mind that Lightfoot felt very solid for such a slight man.

"My God, Lightfoot, I thought you were dying."

"Of what?"

"I don't know. Emotional dissociation. What did you yell for?"

"Air. It's stuffy as a faculty meeting in there. Can't I walk around somewhere and clear my head?"

"Anywhere. The penthouse is yours."

"No, outside."

"The balcony?"

"I'm sure I'd fall off the edge. What's wrong with the street?"

"The street isn't shielded. You'd be seen. I built a camouflage shield to cover the top of the building. From outside, from any angle, this looks like an ordinary penthouse apartment. I've kept this setup going for years."

"Then the roof."

"You want to walk around on the roof with the air

conditioning system screaming at you like a dying rhinoceros?"

"Yes. The roof. May I take the document with me?"

Luthor had Lightfoot and the precious papers with their torn lead casing escorted to the roof and left alone. Moments later a swirl of colors spun into the smiling form of Towbee. Lightfoot handed the document to the elf and with a splash of discordant sound the little philologist disintegrated into the instrument from which he had emerged just hours ago.

Towbee took the time to materialize at the desks of several unstrung news reporters to inform them that he did not appreciate the manner in which art was vulgarly hawked on this planet.

"My outrage grows each hour I stay;
I'll leave your Earth without delay."

And he did.

Sometime during the latter five to ten minutes of the news broadcast the apparent size of the studio crew and staff began to increase. On a closer examination it became obvious that these added "staff" were not doing much of anything beyond standing around, gossiping, watching the show, that sort of thing. Unlike entertainment shows, the news always had lots of background chatter. It was thought that this lent the atmosphere of a newsroom to the broadcast.

The new people included most of the staff of the *Daily Planet* left in the building, as well as secretaries, night receptionists, agents, and executive types from the various enterprises of Galaxy communications; recording, opinion polling, publishing, entertainment, merchandising, and so forth. At first they came because word of free drinks and food started to trickle through the elevator shafts. Now they came mostly to watch what Lois Lane called *The Steve and Clarkie Show*.

"Not once, you say. Not once in your whole life, you say. Is that right, Clarkie?" The sportscaster hung over the back of his chair much as his loosened tie drooped from his neck. He was halfway through his second Bloody Mary.

"Never, I told you. Is that so incredible?" Not a single bead of sweat surfaced on Clark Kent's face during a broadcast or after one, or at any other time, for that matter. He made up for that chink in the armor of his identity by dropping papers now and then as he cleared news copy off his desk, then bending as awkwardly as feasible to pick them up.

"You heard him, everyone. Anyone else here never do it even once? C'mon, don't be shy." Those who thought Lombard went beyond the realm of clowning into indecency seemed to outnumber those who were amused. *The Steve and Clarkie Show* still apparently had the most loyal audience in town. "Hah! At least, no one else's gonna admit to it in public."

"Actually, I always thought it was a rather admirable quality to avoid that sort of thing."

"You're from a farm town. How about the hayloft?"

"Never."

"In back of the VFW hall during a square dance?"

"Not then, either."

"Down by the lake when the folks were off cornhusking? Under the bleachers in high school? At the back gate during lunch hour? In study hall?"

"During school hours? My dad'd tan my hide."

"His dad. Hear that? Good old dad." Lombard held out his half-finished tumbler of vodka and tomato juice. "I mean I can't believe that you lived in the Land of the

Free all your life and never touched an ounce of booze."

During his career in professional football Steve Lombard carefully cultivated the reputation of a partier. Now his growing belly and barrel chest that made pinstriped shirts contour like a bulging jail cell did it for him.

"Seems to me there were a few years back there when it was illegal to drink alcohol in the Land of the Free."

"Prohibition? Ancient history. Nobody took that law seriously. You always ignore dumb laws. It's the American way."

Lois saw Clark foundering. He always foundered when he was about to be winning. "Hey, hundred-thousand-dollar man," she yelled from beside Benny's snack cart, "talking about ignoring dumb laws, what'd you pay in taxes last year?"

The lady customarily brought the house down.

"Lissentame, Clarkie." Lombard took control again. "Howboutchew take a gulpa this baby, huh?" He held out his drink.

"No, thanks." Clark, of course, was nursing a container of chocolate milk.

"Whadja do for drinks, anyway?"

"When I was a kid? Well, Ma had this concoction she used to make. Like nectar of the gods."

"Now we're gettin' somewhere. Did she have a still out back, too?"

"No no no. She put in pineapple juice and apple juice and orange juice and a pinch of curry and some other things. It was the finest tasting liquid nourishment in the world. Probably the whole Solar System."

"The hell it was. This here Bloody Mary's got it beat. Any Bloody Mary's got it beat."

"Nothing's got it beat."

"Wanna make a little wager on that, Clarkie?"

Now Lombard had him. Everyone in the studio was

115

cheering and stomping and yelling "Bet!" or "Put your money where your mouth is," or something similarly appropriate.

"No bet," Clark protested. "I never bet."

" 'Fraid you're gonna lose, eh, Clarkie?"

"I won't lose. Even you'd say the concoction tastes better than a Bloody whatever her name is."

"Then you'll bet. A week's salary?"

"No, I don't bet money." Hisses from the bleachers.

"How about food? Do you bet food? Dinner? If three unprejudiced people pick your soft drink over the Bloody Mary, I treat you to supper anywhere in town you say. If I win, it's your treat."

"Well, that sounds fair, but—" Cries of "chickengut" and "waffler" from the chorus.

"Then it's a bet. You heard it, folks. And maybe we'll even get to see Mr. Kent's virgin throat moistened by a splash of the juice, hey?"

From the back of the studio a very prim young lady stuck her head in the door. She had that caged look of a receptionist still on duty. "Mr. Kent, telephone."

Clark took the chance to bolt from his seat and plow through friends and acquaintances out of the room to the young lady as Steve swayed through a monologue about the evils of abstinence. "Who is it?" Clark asked her. "Something important?"

"I don't know. It's on your private line. He says he's Lex Luthor, and he does a really good imitation of his voice."

Sharp shooting pains to the stomach. In Clark's most persistent nightmare, Luthor finds out his secret identity and devises a way to announce it to everyone in the world except Superman himself. Clark wakes up in the morning, in his dream, to cheering crowds outside the window of his third-floor apartment at 344 Clinton Street. He opens the hallway door and finds shoulder-to-shoulder admirers blocking the path to the elevator. People flock to Metropolis and jam the hotels and park benches and subway tunnels. The ratings on his local news show break national records. Women wherever he goes, even at work, throw their bodies in his path. People jump out of windows and leap in front of moving trucks when they see him in order to attract his attention. A smiling Morgan Edge tries to ingratiate himself by giving Clark a million-dollar-a-year raise. He has to be Superman all the time. It is hellish.

"Hello?" Clark said.

"Hello, Kent."

It was Luthor, not a mimic. The voiceprint was unmistakeable. "Yes, this is Clark Kent. Who is this?"

"It's Luthor, Kent. Listen, you'll tell your friend Superman I'm madder than I've ever been at anyone since the day that super-powered bonehead made me lose my hair. It's been stolen."

"Your hair?"

"No you sparrow-brain. The document."

"Document?"

"The Einstein papers. The stuff I lifted from that vault the other day. It was the feature story on your show, or don't you pay attention to what you're reading?"

"Yes. Yes, I know. But I thought you stole it, didn't you?"

"Not this time, you dolt. It was stolen from me. My mind, this is like trying to talk with a grapefruit."

"You don't have to get insulting, Mr. Luthor. Why did you call me?" Clark was going through the tedious process of tracing the call with x-ray vision.

"To tell you where your friend Superman can find me."

"Oh," Clark said as if replying to the question, what's the fifteenth letter of the alphabet? "Where?" He would

117

stimulate an electron in the wire with x-ray vision, watch the impulse travel a few feet or a few inches until it hit an intersection of two wires.

"Tonight at Pier 82. The slip where they dock those tourist boats."

"Tonight . . . tourist boats . . ." He would then send an impulse down each of the intersecting wires, and one of them would dash back at Clark's phone with the speed of light. He kept following these impulses in trial-and-error fashion until now he traced his connection for three blocks.

"I'll be on the bridge of the ship called *The New Atlantis* at nine-thirty tonight. Can you get in touch with him by then?"

"I can try." His impulse was coming from twelve blocks away now, and that looked to be more than half-way to Luthor's location.

"I'll help him find the thief of the papers. Tell him just to be cool, I'm not going to pull anything. I won't have them snatched out of my hands like—"

"Excuse me, but would you hold on while I get a pencil to write this all down?" He'd found Luthor. He was in a telephone booth at the corner of St. Marks Place and First Avenue.

"You mean you don't have—you weren't writing this down when I told you?"

"No, please hold on."

Luthor was fit for a pen at the zoo. "You screaming dumbo, Kent. If there's one thing I can't abide in people who manage to get as successful as you, it's incompetence. If you worked for me I'd—*yiiii!*"

Luthor was up in the air. Phone booth and all. Thirty feet off the ground and held aloft by a flying figure trailing a red cape.

"Hello? Hello, Mr. Luthor?" came the voice from the

118

dropped receiver as thick telephone cable unwound after the rising booth from below the street.

"Hello, are you still there? Mr. Luthor?" came the words from Superman's throat, projected by super-ventriloquism through the receiver until the instant the cable snapped at the floor of the phone booth. He set his burden on the roof of a three-story building with a cleaning shop on the ground floor. Superman had no need to ask the first question.

"He stole it. He stole it, the little twerp Lightfoot snapped it out from under my nose like an apple off a cart."

"Lightfoot?" Superman joined Luthor's conversation.

"John Lightfoot. The crooked philologist."

"He must've done it before yesterday, old man. He's very dead."

"He's not dead. He made it out of the crash. He was here in Metropolis, and he stole it."

"Hate to contradict you, but I saw him before the police got there. I would have gotten there first, too, if he hadn't died almost instantly. It was quite horrible."

"You saw him? Dead?"

"I did."

"Then who—" Luthor fell silent and thoughtful and built up to his late mood by degrees across the words: "Who stole my document!"

"You'll tell me all about it on the way to your favorite jail cell upstate."

"You don't want to take me back to jail. I'll help you find it. I want the document found."

"Trust me. I'll find it. Next time, figure out another story." The Kryptonian grabbed for Luthor's arm.

Luthor yanked back his other arm, pulling back something in his pocket. A spark leaped at Superman's hand as he touched Luthor. "I said listen to me."

119

"Ouch. What was that?"

"An electrical charge strong enough to take out the whole Metropolis Police Department and a couple of platoons of Marines, if necessary. Unfortunately it affects you like a sudden attack from a bubble bath."

"No more tricks. Come on and—"

"No, dammit! Listen to me. Don't you understand? Don't you see? I won't allow it."

"Tell me about it on the way up to—"

"Keep your paws off me, freak!" He pulled a tiny lead-encased pistol from that pocket and Superman froze. "I'm not ready for a fight, but you know I can put one up. I'll use this if I have to."

Superman could not see what the gun was. His x-ray vision, like any radiation, was unable to penetrate the heavy metal lead. He was wary. There was nowhere Luthor could go, although the criminal had fooled him before.

"This stuff was just to get out of any tight spots in case some over-eager cop recognized me on the street. I won't fight you. I just want to tell you I won't have *his* papers falling into the hands of a . . . a philistine."

"Just take it easy there, Luthor. You probably can't hurt me, but we're in the middle of a crowded city. Einstein, you mean? It's Einstein you're talking about?"

"*His* words. I won't allow it. And don't talk to me like some pimple-faced kid with a zip gun. I'm a pro."

"Offhand I'd say you already allowed it. I wouldn't have thought Einstein was one of your big heroes."

"Who did you think were my heroes, you pigeon-brained muscleman? Capone? Hitler? You? What do you take me for?"

"An escaped felon." In less than the blink of an eye Luthor suddenly saw his weapon lying at his feet and felt his arms being held motionless from behind him. The voice came from behind now, too. "And a misguided man,

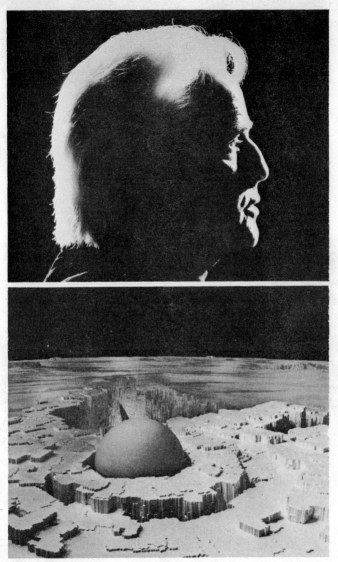

Jor-El (Marlon Brando), the most brilliant scientific mind of the planet Krypton's Council of Elders, which meets in the great dome in the heart of the beautiful crystal city of Kryptonopolis.

Jor-El testifies at the trial of General Zod, Non, and Ursa (Terence Stamp, Jack O'Halloran, Sarah Douglas), who had sought to overthrow the government of Krypton. The Council banishes the three villains to eternal imprisonment in the Phantom Zone of space.

Left, top to bottom: The Council dispatches a police officer to prevent Jor-El from leaving the doomed planet; in his laboratory, Jor-El and his wife, Lara (Susannah York), unable to leave themselves, place their son, Kal-El, in a tiny starship and bid him farewell.

Right: The starship rises, beginning the long journey toward Earth.

Above: The starship rises above Krypton. **Below:** The destruction of Krypton brings death to Jor-El and Lara. **Right, top to bottom:** The starship lands, burning a path across a Kansas wheatfield. Kal-El emerges before the astonished eyes of Jonathan and Martha Kent (Glenn Ford, Phyllis Thaxter), then astounds them further with a display of his prodigious strength.

Top to bottom: Jonathan Kent reflects on the happiness brought by Kal-El, now his adopted son Clark. After Jonathan's funeral, Clark accepts his destiny and tells Martha Kent that he must leave her. In the arctic wasteland, Clark builds the mighty Fortress of Solitude; there, in his first appearance as Superman, he confronts the enduring spirit of his father, Jor-El.

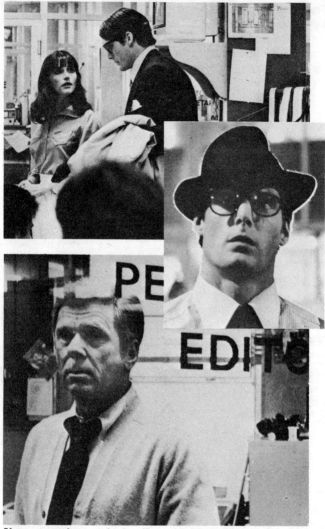

Above, top to bottom: At the offices of the **Daily Planet,** mild-mannered reporter Clark Kent meets fellow reporter Lois Lane (Margot Kidder) and his new boss, editor Perry White (Jackie Cooper). **Right:** The **Daily Planet** helicopter crashes on its rooftop pad—and Lois Lane, jolted from her seat, hangs on and screams for help.

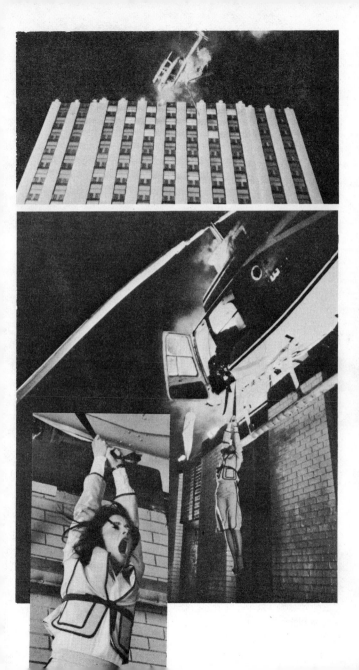

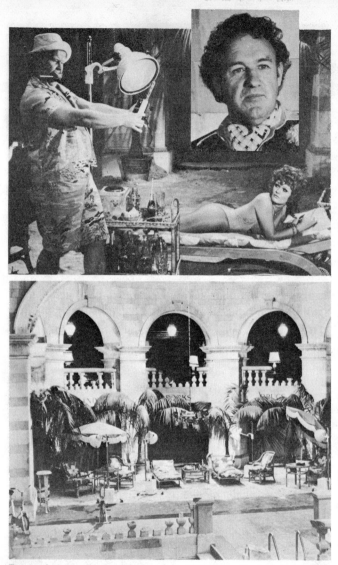

Top to bottom: The villainous Lex Luthor (Gene Hackman); Luthor's henchman, Otis (Ned Beatty), is a puzzlement to henchwoman Eve Teschmacher (Valerie Perrine); the lunatic luxury of Luthor's underground lair.

Top to bottom: On a country road in Colorado, a military convoy escorts the great XK101 rocket; eager soldiers rush to Eve's aid after her faked accident; Luthor, disguised as a doctor, whispers instructions to the seductive decoy.

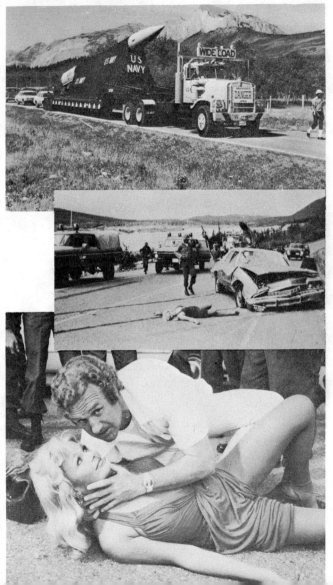

Luthor's villainy has burst Hoover Dam and parted railroad tracks, but Superman copes. **Bottom:** Underground and underwater, he repairs the crumbling dam. **Top:** He spans the gap in the tracks, so that the train can pass safely over him.

Superman's work is never done.
Calm and confident, he faces the great tasks ahead.

your heroes notwithstanding. What is that thing on the floor?"

Luthor let out a resigned breath. "A pipe lighter, if you must know."

"Let's go." Superman scooped the criminal up in both arms for a 35-minute flight of slightly less than sixty miles. Luthor caught a cold.

16

Oa

In a dark patch of space at the core of the brilliant Central Cluster, on a planetoid called Oa, sit the oldest humanoids in the Galaxy. They touch the existence of thousands of trillions of intelligent races, most of whom know them simply, in languages and dialects defying count, as the Guardians.

Average humanoid height in the Galaxy was somewhere between two and two-and-a-half meters. The nine Guardians were all an identical height of 124 centimeters. They also had filtrums.

Filtrums are rectangular clefts in the skin leading from

the bridge between the two nostrils to the middle of the upper lip. Most of the humanoids in the area of the Central Cluster had them. The only known incidences of filtrums in humanoids outside that region of the Galaxy were on the planets Earth and Krypton. There were several theories on the reasons for this incidence of the apparently functionless birthmark, but one thing was known about them. Only humanoids with filtrums were capable of smiling.

The youngest of the Guardians was born within twenty years of the oldest, roughly eight billion years ago. Their blue skin was completely unwrinkled, they no longer had visible pores or prints in their skin, they each had a fringe of thick white fur around the sides and backs of their heads, they were virtually identical in appearance. What active communication they had with each other was instant, on a subliminal level. They no longer had any need for telepathy. Their functions were identical, their aspirations and jealousies were lost to the ages. Only one Guardian had actually left Oa in eight billion years, and he returned only briefly to be stripped of his immortality as punishment for some subtle breach of the group's ethical code.

Somewhere in the labyrinthine tunnels and towers and interconnecting halls of the Guardians' headquarters on the otherwise barren planetoid, two of the immortals were communicating.

Our wayward brother has located and induced a dream sleep upon the Earthman, the first Guardian told the second.

Is he equipped to feed tomorrow's experiences into the mind of the Terran? the second inquired of the first.

He will be, by the time our evaluation of his interview with the woman arrives at Earth.

The second Guardian passed his hand over a light on the wall as a spotlight from the ceiling bathed the first

Guardian's head, feeding information directly into the immortal's mind.

The light went off as the Guardian integrated the information and noted, I believe you have done a good job, but I have one possible improvement.

Might I consider it? the second suggested without apprehension.

The point at which the woman Lane asks, Have you ever tried to talk a mugger out of pursuing his vocation, Professor Gordon?

Yes, where the man Gordon responds, I haven't had the opportunity, thank the stars.

Exactly. It is with the response that I have a question. Perhaps he could respond with an attempt at levity. For example, God parted the Red Sea for Moses, the Colonials beat back the British Empire, the Mets won the pennant in '69, and a mugger can be talked down, Miss Lane.

That is quite in keeping with the Terran penchant for light humor, and I considered such a response, but I determined that in Professor Gordon's case it would be out of character.

I concede to your superior acquaintance with the subject. I shall begin to feed the experience into the young man's somnolent mind. He will believe himself to have been functional during this entire period.

17

The Sociologist

After Superman had left Luthor in the prison in Pocantico, Clark Kent made one more appearance in Studio B so that he could be roped firmly into his bet with Steve Lombard—and in Lois Lane's office so that he could make a lunch date for the following afternoon. Superman was busier.

Clark was walking down the sixth-floor hallway with Jimmy Olsen toward the elevator, and he accepted the offer of a ride to his apartment in Jimmy's new TR7. In a moment Clark's time sync changed, as it occasionally did.

"Listen, Jimmy. Let me take a raincheck on that ride home. I think I'll walk."

"Yeah, sure, Clark. Watch out for the wall. Hey, where you running? You sure are in a hurry to take a leisurely stroll uptown." By now Jimmy was talking to himself.

Less than a minute later a whistling filled the air

over an uncommonly choppy Lake Superior and crew members near panic on a threatened cargo ship looked up into the sky. Then all fifty-two of them fell flat on the deck, holding onto their shifting centers of gravity as the big ship was lifted forty feet into the air and flown to port.

On the way back to Metropolis, Superman spotted an ambulance with its siren whirring and red light spinning, stranded immobile in the middle lane of Route 80 between Totowa and Fairfield, New Jersey. He lifted this stranded ship out of dead calm seas and delivered it to the hospital whose name was on the side. The coronary patient inside was spared the experience by unconsciousness, although an intern taking his electrocardiogram fainted.

In Hillside a cat was stuck in a tree, and her owner was too big to crawl on the branch after her and too small not to cry. At the instant Superman heard the cat yowl, the wrist of a young woman on Greene Street in Metropolis was grabbed by a man who had been waiting in one of the standard dark alleys peppering the neighborhood.

"Hey, man, what're you doin?" the girl squeaked.

"Come in here, you."

A beam of heat vision snapped the branch of the tree and the cat fell.

"Get your hand off me or—"

"Or what? Whatcha got there, girlie?"

She calmed down and found her misplaced equilibrium. "Listen, man, why doncha buy me a drink and do it right?"

A thin stream of super breath from above bounced off the concrete and softened the kitten's four-legged landing.

"I mean, why do you wanna force yourself on a girl like that, hey? I don't bite, do you?"

"Look, don't go tryin' to snow me, girlie," he snarled, but his grip of her arm loosened just a little.

And a blinding streak of red and blue from out of the

125

sky left an indentation on his jaw. In a moment, a bewildered patrolman was dropped out of the sky and the girl gave the cop her account of the incident. The man woke up in a jail cell.

Here are some other things Superman did the night before the full moon:

He melted, confiscated, or otherwise neutralized a collection of knives, chains, and shoddily assembled handguns carried around by a group of twelve teenaged boys roaming through Metropolis Common.

He spun a water current, diverting a school of sharks which were about to attack some tuna congregated around the lifeline to a research bathyscaph. There was every possibility that the sharks would accidentally have severed the line.

With the super pressure of his hands he fused shut a hairline crack that was forming in one of the pontoons underneath Oceania, the experimental floating city 250 miles east of Montauk, Long Island.

He slammed through a half-ton of heroin being loaded onto a ship in Le Havre in four boxes marked "Toys."

He spotted a train in Northern Ireland about to tumble into a canyon through a bridge weakened by saboteurs. He substituted his own body for the weakened portion of rail, and when the train was gone he built a new rail from iron ore and coal he found in nearby deposits.

In northern Greenland he lifted a dogsled, a dozen huskies, a young doctor, and a supply of vital flu serum over an avalanche to a secluded military outpost on the Davis Strait.

Superman spent most of the rest of the night at his Fortress of Solitude carved out of a mountain 130 miles south of the geographic North Pole. There was a gold-colored airline marker pointing the way to the pole, but if one saw the arrow from the bottom—which is something no one but Superman ever did—it became apparent that this was the 30-ton key to a door camouflaged by the constant inclement weather and the indented face of the mountain. In the fortress the Man of Steel checked bacterial cultures with which he experimented. He was no medical genius, but he did, after all, have immediate total recall and he was the only being of whom he knew who could safely handle the Regulus-243 strain which caused a violent chemical reaction in organic matter, turning it on contact into particles of a saline crystal. Superman occasionally wondered if the only recorded incidence of Regulus-243 contamination on Earth was the death of Lot's wife during the destruction of Sodom and Gomorrah.

Superman fed and groomed the fearsome menagerie of domesticated extraterrestrial creatures he kept and studied in one of the lower levels of the fortress. He wrote an entry, in the Kryptonese language, in his personal journal. He painted a landscape in acrylics—he favored the vistas of Jupiter and its moons, but this was a Martian plain—while he listened to a recording of sonic flare patterns as performed by a musician of Polaris-4.

He slept for half an hour, which was something he did because he needed a certain amount of dreaming to maintain a psychological balance. Then he took off, straight up, to plunge through the molten crust of the sun 93 million miles away in order to sterilize himself. It would be bad form, after all, to carry any Regulus-243 cells back to Metropolis.

It was a bit under seventeen minutes to the sun and back traveling at the speed of light—which was the fastest he could travel through "real" three-dimensional space. He looked down as dawn hit Metropolis. Morgan Edge was sprawled on the fold-out couch in his office. For a multimillionaire he certainly didn't allow himself much recreation. Jimmy was just arriving home after a long night of rigorous leisure. Steve Lombard was not at home, and Superman could not begin to wonder about where he might be. Lois had been awake for at least an hour. It had to have taken at least that long to get from her apartment to the subway car on which Superman found her. She was up to something.

Superman kept a telescopic x-ray eye on the lady as he landed on the roof of the apartment building at 344 Clinton Street. He scanned the sky for planes overhead. Once a Soviet satellite 103 miles up took a picture as he was changing to Clark Kent. A crew of technicians wasted a week before the Russians decided it wasn't worth the effort to find out how film could be overexposed in the void of space.

As Clark Kent walked down the roof stairway to the thirty-third-floor landing, Lois's train was pulling into the old World's Fair grounds, the last stop on that line. As she stepped off the train he stepped into the elevator and pushed the button for the third floor. As he stepped off the elevator she walked down the stairway toward the subway graveyard where hundreds of inanimate subway cars lay in wait for rush hour or the scrap heap, vulnerable to the inarticulate expression of graffiti artists armed with spray paint.

Clark Kent walked down the third-floor corridor and unlocked the door of apartment 3-D, twisting his neck in the opposite direction all the way. He stepped inside, closed the door behind him, loosened his tie, opened his shirt, dropped his jacket and glasses on a chair, and put two eggs up to boil.

Lois Lane squeezed through a rip in the hurricane fence and counted the rows of subway cars. She tried to remember which car her source had told her to check. It was too hot a piece of information to write down. She found the seventh row and counted sixteen cars in the direction away from the fairgrounds. She crept between the ranks of cars to her target and pulled a stethoscope from her purse. She fitted it to her ears and listened to the hull of the train.

Clark picked at his eggs and buttered toast. Breakfast was a habit from his school days. He sat in his living room reclining chair as he peered across town.

Lois surely enough heard voices inside the subway car, although she could make out only snatches of the conversation. She heard things like, "last night's shipment . . . backfire soon as shoot . . . street value . . . sixty bucks a piece . . . move them by noon tomorrow . . . every high school in the city . . ."

Clark Kent looked through the wall of the subway car and found three men standing over two crates filled with cheaply manufactured handguns. He counted 288 pistols in the crates. A tall man in a three-piece suit was handing an attaché case filled with cash to another man in the uniform of a subway signalman.

Lois Lane had heard enough. She stuffed the stethoscope into her shoulder bag and tripped backward over a pile of discarded spray paint cans. She froze at the noise, crawled under the subway car, and waited there for a few minutes. They hadn't heard her, or thought anything of it if they had. She pulled herself, more warily now, out from under the train and made her way back toward the rip in the fence.

Clark Kent was no longer in the apartment.

First Lois would call Inspector Henderson. Bill was one cop who understood the concept of privileged information and he knew how to keep a story quiet until it was revealed to the world by a deserving reporter. Then she would call the *Daily Planet* city desk and tell them to leave a good-sized hole in the upper-left corner of page one. Then she would call WGBS News and have someone drive out here to the backwoods of the city with a change of clothes and a portable typewriter. Then a hand grabbed her around the throat and threw her to the ground.

The two men stood over Lois with guns pointed at her face. These would be real guns, not the explosive Tinkertoys they were planning to sell to the children of Metropolis.

"All right, whaddya know, lady?"

No answer.

"Don't I know you?" the other one said.

Silence.

"Who told you where we'd be? You a cop?"

"Hey, she's no cop. She's a reporter." A hint of mortal fear in his voice.

"How d'you know?"

"I recognize her. Hey, we better get outta here."

"Are you nuts? Frisk her."

"Not me. That broad's got her own portable bodyguard."

"You're talkin' crazy. If you won't frisk her, I—" The man's pistol drooped like a wilting plant. The molten steel that used to be part of the stock left third-degree burns on his hand. He dropped to the ground screaming until he fell unconscious.

The other man tore off in the direction of the hole in the fence. Twenty feet before he got there, he ran into a colorful immoveable object and crumpled.

"Miss Lane, do you come here often?" Superman asked.

She thought to say that she could have gotten out of this fix herself. That she'd left a sealed envelope in Perry's Office, and that it would be opened if she wasn't at the office by ten. That maybe Superman was a little rough on those two. That it would have been nice to deserve credit for mashing a mass sale of Saturday Night Specials herself. But there he was, standing there . . .

130

Smiling.

"You've got to live until at least noon, Lois. I doubt Clark could handle that highbrow social theorist on his own."

He glowed with life and power, and sometimes he twinkled under the sun. He was a fallen star. She thought that all the time, but of course she couldn't say it. The phrase would be out of character. What she could do was hug him so hard he might feel the pressure and maybe he would kiss her.

The young man puffed serenely on his bent pipe and tried hard to explain the concept so that his interviewer could understand. "There was an illustration of my point on the radio news only this morning," Fellman Gordon said.

Camera 3 dollied in for a closeup of the sociologist.

"I heard an interview with a young lady," Gordon said, "who was allegedly saved by Superman from an assault attempt only last night."

Lois sat in the interviewer's chair. "Superman turned up lots of places last night. We reporters have noticed that there's a spate of unlikely reports for about three days every month or so. He supposedly does everything from fighting back an invasion of flying saucers over Mongolia to helping children with their long division, apparently at the same time."

"This happens to be a documented report. It was witnessed not only by the victim but by a police officer. A young lady of about twenty claims she had nearly persuaded a mugger to leave her alone when Superman intervened out of nowhere to save her."

"Have you ever tried talking a mugger out of pursuing his vocation, Professor Gordon?"

"I haven't had the opportunity, thank the stars, but neither did that young lady. Before she could get out of

131

trouble herself, Superman saved her. What he has done, I believe, is ended despair."

Clark Kent, watching the taping of *Sunday Forum* from the control booth with the director, needed no cues to keep a blank look on his face.

"It is my contention, and I expound upon this in my book, *Age of Dependence*," Fellman Gordon continued, "that Superman may be singlehandedly bringing the social development of our entire human race to a grinding halt."

"How do you explain the strides over the past twenty years in science? Space exploration? Food production?"

"These are not social phenomena. They are scientific and, to some extent, political developments. Let me give you a hypothetical case, Miss Lane. You, it is well known, have a sort of personal relationship with Superman. I take it he has actually saved your life more times than you can count."

"I'm perfectly capable of counting that high, it's just that I wasn't keeping score." It was a lame crack, but it helped Lois avoid blushing.

"Say you were somewhere really out of the way, Miss Lane. In Zaire. In the abandoned shaft of a diamond mine. The mine caved in. You had about an hour's supply of air. Absolutely no one knew where you were, and even if they did there would be no chance of getting you out in time. What goes through your mind?"

"I wish Superman would stop stalling. I've got a deadline to meet."

"Exactly. You don't make your peace with your God or your conscience. You don't cry. You don't go mad. You wait impatiently for Superman to save you. That possibility now exists. No one need despair any more. Superman plays adopted father to the world, ready to bail anyone out of trouble the way his father Jor-El bailed him out of a dying planet. The only evidence of significant social growth over the past ten years, I have found, has been among those outside law-abiding society."

Where would someone like Luthor be if Superman had never come to Earth? Probably, Gordon supposed, in a research laboratory somewhere discovering a cure for cancer. Or maybe in a mental institution following a childhood spent in a succession of reform schools. Certainly there would have been no consuming ambition, no enemy impossible to overcome, to teach him to aspire. Without Superman, Luthor might have grown up lonely. And what of the occasional outlandish creatures from outer space who happen to touch down in Metropolis to pick a fight with him every so often? If Superman had never come, would Earth people even be aware that there was life elsewhere in the Universe? Maybe we knew too soon, before we were strong enough to face the interlocking cultures of the Galaxy on equal terms. It was taken for granted in scientific and political circles that one day the people of Earth would compete for power and recognition among Galactic society as did any young civilization reaching into space. Would we really be equipped to do that when the time came?

It was an idea that Clark Kent pondered occasionally. No one had ever expressed it publicly before; maybe no one else had bothered to think of it before Fellman Gordon. Well, now it was in print and that was just as well, Clark thought. It was.

After the taping Lois grinned at Clark in the booth with that we-know-something-this-guy-doesn't-know grin. Clark wondered what it was he and Lois both knew. The only concern of the director was the fact that the show ran an extra thirty seconds and that would have to be edited out. Fellman Gordon followed Clark down the hallway toward Clark's office.

Gordon didn't call to Clark, so the newsman didn't turn

around to see why he was being followed. The sociologist was a dark man in his early thirties, of medium height and build. He wore a mustache that was trimmed so as to look unkempt. As Clark walked he perceived a slight change in the quality of Gordon's footsteps, a lightening somehow. As he reached the office the voice came from behind Clark.

"Kal-El, may I speak with you a moment?"

Clark turned around and where Fellman Gordon belonged there stood one of the immortal Guardians.

18

Old-Timer

Clark Kent closed the office door behind himself and his visitor, leaned back in his chair, and allowed himself to smile Superman's smile. If anyone barged in at that moment, the glasses and blue suit would be no disguise.

"First question," Superman's smile asked, "are you really here or are you some kind of astral projection? I thought you fellows didn't leave Oa."

"I am very real, Kal-El. You may notice that my skin is nearly as peach-colored as yours, a bit browner like the humanoids of Malthus, the world of the Guardians' birth."

"I assumed that was part of your disguise."

"Regrettably not. You see I am no longer immortal. If you observe you may notice that I have skin pores, also, and look." The ancient pressed his palm on Clark's desk, "I leave fingerprints, as well."

"You're the Old-Timer. The Guardian fallen from grace."

"I am."

"All right. The obvious question is, where's the real Fellman Gordon?"

"Asleep in his home. I have already caused his mind to experience the events which I live today in his identity. He will awaken this evening after what he felt to be an afternoon nap, and he will be most pleased tomorrow when he watches the broadcast of Miss Lane's interview of him."

"Don't tell me the answer to my next question. I'll tell you. The reason you came here designed as Fellman Gordon was that the sociologist has stumbled upon some Universal Truth and you wanted to emphasize it to me and the television audience so that the message comes across properly."

"He approached a new idea, at least new for the civilization of Earth. I should like to point it out for you—that for every social force there is an equal and opposite social force, that we each live in vibratory patterns, and that the only reason we do not discern these patterns as readily as we see the patterns we live in as readily as we see radio waves or the ripples left by a pebble in water is that the frequencies we travel are too large to measure in one human lifetime."

Clark lost his Superman smile quite unconsciously. He

tried very hard, every time he encountered one of these aged beings, not to be as impressed as he was the last time. Clark had no idea how the contention that his presence interfered with Earth's social growth evolved into the concept of vibratory patterns and frequencies and immortality and the role of humankind in a complex and confusing Universe. He didn't pursue the question.

"These are merely tertiary matters," the Old-Timer said, as if taking Clark's faded smile as a cue to get to business. "You have been concerned recently with an epistle left by your eminent Professor Einstein."

Clark was startled again. "What was in the document? What do you know about Einstein?"

"A bit more, I suspect, than you do. We took quite an active interest in his career."

"Where can I find the document?"

"In the custody of the Master of Oric."

"Oric. Fourth planet of the Vega system. I've never been there, it's a blue star sun. Isn't that the home planet of Towbee the space minstrel?"

"That is by all accounts the place of his birth."

"Was he the thief?"

"That would be a logical suspicion."

"What do you suggest I do?"

"You have reduced powers, Kal-El, on a planet whose star sun is blue. Your optical abilities are restricted and your invulnerability to physical assault is not as apparently limitless. You have no familiarity with the planet, whose technology and consequent dangers to you draw on contributions from nearly a thousand independent cultures from hundreds of light-years away. Your unknown adversary, the Master, is apparently particularly interested in some supposed discovery of Einstein's. It would be advisable, therefore, for you to go to Oric with an assistant who qualifies as a creative technician of the first magnitude as well as an expert on Einsteinian physics."

Predictably, Clark/Superman could not dispute the Old-Timer's logic.

The night of the full moon, Superman quietly incapacitated a hired hit-man who was on his way to Lois Lane's apartment. He had the assassin charged with major offenses unrelated to Lois, for which he guaranteed proof within the week. Superman also raced midnight over half the globe, foiling a jewelry robbery in Marseilles and destroying a footbridge in Rhodesia before a group of armed civilian raiders could cross to a racially segregated area in order to incite a disturbance. He rescued a child falling from a third-floor window in Liberia. He anonymously whipped up an easterly wind to help a seventeen-year-old boy trying to sail across a becalmed Atlantic Ocean on the last leg of a solo voyage around the world. He located the twin daughters of an Argentinian government official in the apartment of a kidnapper and spirited them home minutes before police arrived on the scene, so that the kidnapper could not negotiate an escape using his hostages. In Baja California he dragged two cars, stranded in the same desolate mudhole, back to a major artery and then compacted the mudhole to the consistency of asphalt. On the southeastern outskirts of San Francisco he dived underground to ease the pressure on a certain section of the San Andreas Fault and delay the inevitable earthquake for another month or so. In Alaska he fused shut a growing leak in the central portion of the oil pipeline and burned up the black mess that had leaked over the wilderness before anyone saw it. When he was 130 miles south of the North Pole, he wrote an entry in his journal. Then Superman leaped seventeen hundred miles into the Aurora Borealis and saw the day's first hint of sunlight on the eastern horizon. He dived like a missile at Washington, D.C.

Superman landed noiselessly on the Truman Balcony of the White House. There, unnoticed, he slept for nearly

137

an hour, until he was awakened before dawn by the sound of the President of the United States brushing his remarkable collection of teeth.

19

Pocantico To Vega

Lex Luthor did not sleep the way most people slept. Experience had taught prison officials how unwise it was to allow their star inmate unsupervised access to tools or chemical materials of any kind. The only objects in Luthor's cell after ten o'clock lights out were a legal pad and a ball-point pen. This was a foolish precaution, of course. The prison would hold Luthor for as long as Luthor chose to be held, and not a moment longer. Meanwhile, B.J. was perfectly capable of seeing that the boss's diverse enterprises did not crumble in his absence.

One night, in a loose moment, Luthor figured out how to melt the plastic cap of the pen, let a certain amount drip into the ink refill, extract a substance from the glue that bound the legal pad, wrap it all in half a sheet of yellow paper and make an explosive powerful enough to blast out a wall of his cell. Luthor would never do that, of course. If he did, the next time he was in jail the warden wouldn't give him his pen and pad.

Luthor was adept at writing in the dark. He would sleep for a minute, or an hour or two, or not at all, and as an idea struck him he would scrawl it on a clean sheet of yellow paper. He replaced his pad about twice a week. This was a particularly productive night, for his cold kept him from sleeping. From the position of the full moon that shone through the window opposite his cell it looked to be about 6:10 in the morning. On the eighth page of a pad that was new when night fell Luthor drew by moonlight a sketch for a new kind of barometer whose design was based on the shell configuration of a certain extinct mollusk. Then a shadow fell over the moon.

"I need your help, Lex," said the startling, reverberant voice of the shadow.

"You." The reaction wasn't clever, but its tone was eloquent enough.

"I've cleared it with the warden and the Justice Department," Superman explained. "We can leave immediately and the next time the Parole Board meets, your release will be granted retroactively."

"What do you want me to do, microbe-head? Teach you how to tie a shoe without missing and putting your hand through the floor?"

"This is important."

"I know. If your shoe falls off while you're flying faster than sound it could go into orbit and somebody at the Federal Aviation Administration would have to fill out a form in triplicate."

"Will you calm down? There are people sleeping."

"What's the matter? They're all heinous criminals. Bank robbers. Jaywalkers. Potential Nobel Prize winners. Hey, do you want to see how a Kryptonian ties his shoe?"

"Lex."

"He does it like this." Luthor put his right foot up on his metal cot and bent over to fiddle with his left shoe on the floor. "And what's with the first names, Supe? Soup? May I call you Turkey Noodle?"

"I want to know if you'll accept my terms."

"I've accepted lots of your terms. A term for kidnapping. Six or eight for grand larceny. A couple for sabotage of government property."

"Don't give me a hard time, Luthor. I want you to help me get the Einstein papers back."

"Einstein? Didn't he play Clark Gable's best friend in *Boy Next Door Saves the World?* Big picture about a guy that works in a sporting goods store who finds a secret Nazi code camouflaged on sleeping bag warranty labels. You remember it." Luthor sneezed and gave Superman an opening.

"All right, I've had it. This is what I want. You go with me to a planet circling Vega where the document is now, and you help me get it back. For that you get either a parole or transportation anywhere in the Galaxy you feel like settling down. Take it or leave it."

"Make it a full Presidential pardon and you've got a deal."

"That's a pretty stiff order."

"You can do it, you're Superman."

"That's true." The big man produced a document from the pouch in the lining of his cape. It was a pardon for all federal offenses—the only ones with which any prosecutor thought it necessary to charge Luthor—effective immediately. It was signed not half an hour earlier by the President and the Attorney General.

"This won't change anything, you know," Luthor said.

Superman said, "I know."

Superboy was impressed by the increasingly erratic nature of Lex's behavior even before the Jefferson-Baker

Science Contest. The young hero was even more impressed, though, by the hologram project in progress and supposed that Lex's behavior was part of the pressure that comes from the process of creation. There is a high incidence of emotional instability, Superboy knew, among people in creative fields like the one Lex was clearly entering. This deviance generally comes to an end, however, when the creator is reinforced by recognition. When Lex won the Jefferson-Baker scholarship, as he inevitably would, he would once again become the old, moderately tolerable fellow that he was before he became obsessed.

Meanwhile, Lex's aberrations were jarring loose the collective emotional stability of the high school. During the time Lex was building his project he evidently had some trouble creating a holographic image flawless enough to fool people who were standing nearby. His early efforts seemed as though they were flapping in the wind or rippling as if underwater. He thought at first that people might overlook poor quality if what they saw did not appear to be a person standing on a stage, but in a tank of water. One day, when Coach Norm Levine led his first period Smallville High School swimming class into the indoor pool area he saw, lying at the bottom of the pool, the figure of a young brown-haired boy in a crew-neck sweater, smiling cherubically. Alarmed, Coach Levine dove to the bottom of the pool and spent fully a minute and a half grasping at the rippling figure, trying to figure out why he couldn't get hold of it, before he found himself on his back beside the pool with one of his students giving him mouth-to-mouth resuscitation.

A week or so later, in a history class, Miss Carol Roberts asked Lex Luthor what Secretary of State Thomas Jefferson's attitude was toward the Whiskey Rebellion. Lex said that Jefferson was quite adamant in the belief that the federal government should put down any local rebellions before they spread to other areas like a

141

virus. This was, of course, precisely the opposite of Jefferson's feelings and Miss Roberts said so.

"You've obviously been too preoccupied with other things, Lex, since you did not read the assignment. Is there anyone who can tell—"

"Excuse me, Miss Roberts," Lex interrupted, "but I did read the book. I read the whole book the first week of school and I remember just about everything in it."

"I wish you would stay with the class, then, because you've got Jefferson mixed up with Hamilton. Is there someone who—"

"If you look in the book, Miss Roberts,"—Lex was sweet as frosted flakes—"I think you'll find that I'm right."

"Lex Luthor, that's twice in a row you've interrupted me. I think I'll do just that, since you seem so intent on embarrassing yourself. Let me see, that's—"

"Page 213, Miss Roberts."

She would have lost her temper at the third interruption if she weren't so sure of having the last word. "Yes, page 213." The book lay open on her desk and Lex's finger under his desk pressed a pair of wires together as she read:

When asked if he thought Hamilton's actions were wise, Thomas Jefferson said, "If I were Hamilton I would douse the leaders in their own whiskey and set fire to—

Miss Roberts squinted, looked closer at the page and mumbled, "Jefferson couldn't have said anything like—"

She looked up and saw Luthor lose the restraint with which he had held his mouth closed, fall out of his seat and roll on the floor laughing. She sent Lex to the principal's office, looked again at the page of the text which now said something quite different from what she had read aloud, and had trouble finishing sentences for the rest of the day.

Unknown to Lex, Superboy interceded on his behalf on both these occasions. Superboy even asked the principal to ignore it when, following the incident with Miss Roberts, Lex laughed uncontrollably through the first ten minutes of his half-hour detention period, stopped abruptly, mumbled something and, with a wild look in his eyes, ran home for the day. Even Superboy had trouble accepting his behavior the next day when Lex showed up for first-period algebra, red-eyed from lack of sleep. The teacher had asked Lana to do a fairly difficult problem at the board in front of the class, and when she made an error Lex jumped up and screamed something unintelligible. He pushed Lana out of his way, scribbled the solution to the problem and angrily banged a fist on the blackboard, cracking it down the middle of his equation. No one in the room knew quite what to do, so no one moved. Lex stared at all of them during a forbiddingly painful two-and-a-half seconds of utter silence and then howled, "Why do I have to put up with this crap?" He exploded into tears. Clark Kent hopped up to put a hand on Lex's shoulder. Lex hurled away Clark's hand and left the building. His parents didn't see him for two days.

The story goes that Archimedes, for lack of parchment, used to work on the beach, drawing polyhedrons and circles and writing formulas in the sand. During the two days Lex was missing Superboy saw him scrawling in the sand on the shore of Stafford Pond a few miles outside Smallville. One of the two nights Lex spent there he took three hours out to sleep under a clump of bushes, but other than that he did not sleep at all. Almost catatonic, he stared at the lake for hours at a time. He paced. He banged his fists on trees. He laughed. He hid from people who occasionally came by. He cried. He drew intricate diagrams in the sand. Secretly, Superboy uprooted clumps of poison ivy from where Lex might walk in the dark, and otherwise left him alone.

Superboy did not pretend to understand any of this, but he did believe that if the world was lucky, he was witnessing the blooming of a genius. Superboy did not know, Superman did not know, whether genius is a capacity with which some are born, or if it is a product of a peculiar juxtaposition of wonder and terror in a person's education and environment. Whichever was the case, it was happening here and the hero wanted to be sure the process was allowed to run its course. After the contest, Lex came back to the lake and for a week he did very little other than sleep.

Lex was falling asleep, as a matter of fact, when Superboy plucked him off the beach and presented him to his new laboratory. Lex's eyes welled up, he lavished Superboy with thanks and no one saw him for another three weeks.

Some of Lex's classmates and a few of the teachers he had not yet intimidated left food outside the laboratory door. Clark Kent, the only student that the Smallville High faculty trusted not to copy answers that were often more accurate than teachers' answer keys, got the job of leaving Lex's tests and homework in the laboratory mail slot. Some days the food was gone in the morning, but it generally remained. Twice during the two weeks the accumulated assignment pages were tugged in through the mail slot. The next morning, both times, they were in a neat pile, correct and completed, on the ground outside under a basket of rotted fruit. No one ever saw the door open, not ever. Even Superboy had no idea what was going on inside. He had lined the walls and venetian blinds with thin lead sheeting. For three weeks Lex was very like a mystical medieval hermit living in a cave.

Legends say that the First World War was caused by the assassination of Archduke Ferdinand, that an apple

144

falling on the head of Sir Isaac Newton brought about the discovery of gravity, that his murder of an Egyptian slave-master in an instant of righteous madness sent Moses into exile to discover the wonders of God and the desert. The world might be much more orderly and interesting if these things were so, but it is likely that they are not. It is likely that the world would have gone to war had Ferdinand lived, that Newton would have noticed gravity if he had been sitting under a flagpole, that Moses would have recoiled from oppressive Egyptian society even had he witnessed one fewer act of wanton brutality.

When newspapers or magazines publish biographical profiles of Luthor the arch-criminal, when students in social studies classes discuss Superman's greatest enemy on Earth, when convicts who have served time at Pocantico talk about the singular, brooding man with the red-lit eyes, they invariably get around to telling the story of the day he decided to live outside the law, the day the laboratory burned down. Actually, it was coming for a long time.

It was about ten-thirty one night and Lex Luthor appeared outside his laboratory door and yelled, "I did it!"

No one was around to hear him. He had his favorite audience.

"I did it, didja hear? I did it! HOT *DAMN!*"

Smallville went to bed early. Sometimes only Superboy was awake, flying over the village, or over a nearby city, or to the moon if he felt like being even more bored. When Lex took off in a dead run across the field where his laboratory stood, tripped in a rut, rolled over and onto his feet without noticing he had fallen, screamed through the streets howling, "The gametes are coming! The gametes are coming!" Superboy was, in fact, on the moon, staring full-face into the vicious sun, wondering what it meant to be a Superboy, or some such matter teenage boys traditionally ponder. Superboy was going through the familiar

145

identity crisis period of adolescence and was trying very hard not to bother anyone else with it. Today he would learn about guilt.

Lex saw a light in the basement of Kent's General Store and pounded on the door until it opened. Lex expected to see Jonathan Kent, or Clark, being diligent about the books or the inventory or something. Instead, old Whizzer Barnes pulled the door open.

"Hey there, young fella, what're you doing prowling through the streets at this hour?" Whizzer had owned the General Store before Jonathan Kent bought it. He was retired now. He hung a smile from his sagging jowls as he let Lex in. "You're Julie Luthor's boy, right?"

"Yeah, yeah. I'm Lex. Is Clark around?"

"I would think Clark's asleep by now, just like I'd think you ought to be. I was just puttering around in the basement looking for an old records ledger I think I left behind."

"Got any beer? I've gotta celebrate."

"Seems a man can't even do nothing at all if he's of a mind without some government fella asking where he made what money he's living on. You say beer, son?"

"Yeah, like in the fridge or someplace? Mr. Kent must keep something like that around." Lex swung open the door of a deep freeze behind the counter and found only ice cream. "How about tobacco?"

"Ain't been able to get beer in this town since nineteen and fourteen. Before Prohibition."

"Yeah, a corncob pipe. Think Mr. Kent would mind if I grabbed this and paid him for it tomorrow?"

"That was the year they passed the income tax. Folks thought it'd be a good way to keep away the revenuers."

Lex stuffed the pipe in his pocket and clutched a two-ounce pouch of Flying Dutchman tobacco and flew out the door. "Thanks, Mr. Barnes."

"Appears folks was wrong, though."

Whizzer Barnes stood at the open door and stared after Lex for a long time. There was a look behind the boy's eyes he had seen only once before. He couldn't place the look until he remembered an old man who had come into this store—oh, it must have been ten or fifteen years ago. The old man moved slowly, hardly had any cheeks for the wrinkles over his face. He had a mustache, as Whizzer recalled, and had a wool cap pulled down tightly over his head. Lex and the old man didn't move or sound or act the same. What was it about the two of them? Whizzer thought he remembered. The old man had bought a corncob pipe and tobacco too. Whizzer Barnes folded his ledger under an arm and shambled home.

When Superboy entered the atmosphere of the Earth there was smoke seeping out the windows of Lex Luthor's laboratory. Four thousandths of a second later the Boy of Steel crashed through one wall of the structure he had built three weeks earlier and out the opposite wall. The fire, with room to breathe, now spat its killing heat into the open air. Superboy scooped the unconscious Lex Luthor from the floor of the building, wrapped him in his cape to extinguish the flames licking at his clothes and hair and set him down on the open field. When Lex awoke two seconds later, heaving air in and out of his lungs, he saw Superboy emptying his own lungs at Lex's laboratory, his fire, his creation.

Lex raced at the falling building, howling his rage. He got far enough to feel the heat, to need to cover his mouth and nose with a hand as he ran, to feel a hot prickling sensation over his exposed skin, to see the bowlful of living protoplasm he had created with his mind and hands and livid soul die the death that Lex, at that moment, wanted to die.

Searing gas from the combustion of his artificial protoplasm killed the hair follicles of Lex's arms, face and head. Only the hand he was holding over his nose and mouth when Superboy plucked him up, kicking and writhing, for the second time, saved the cilia in his nostrils. He would never grow hair or a beard again. He would laugh or cry or become enraged when pansy philosophers wondered, in the future, whether laboratory life could have a soul. He knew that such life would have no less than the soul of its creator. Lex Luthor chose, from the moment his creation died, to hate the being who had saved his miserable life, who was responsible for the loss of his brown curls and his child. It was the only way he could walk slowly, one millimeter at a time, from the abyss of madness.

Superman came to understand, as Luthor did not, that while Luthor's soul might be as durable as that of any other creature in the Universe, the vulnerable and sensitive body of a mortal can withstand only a certain amount of greatness before it must balance that with venality. Superman occasionally thought to devise some way to give Luthor super-powers, then thought better of it. Luthor was damaged at the same time and with the same terrible efficiency that Superboy had been nurtured. Luthor had never killed a human being, had never been directly responsible for a man or woman's death. The entire mass of his hatred was directed at Superman, who was thankful to take the hatred and leave only Luthor's disdain for the rest of the human community. The Kryptonian became upset whenever he thought of the man who had been his boyhood friend. Superman could only hope that someday God would have mercy on Lex Luthor's tortured soul.

The pair stood outside the walls of the prison as dawn broke, Superman telling what nothing he knew about the situation, Luthor insisting that they should go to Oric separately and that he was perfectly capable of getting there almost as quickly as Superman. For a man with an amazingly creative intellect, who had been turned out of the family by his parents at the age of fifteen, who was completely bald at thirteen, who had no formal education beyond trade school at a juvenile detention home, but who was still considered the world's foremost technical physicist, who had almost never had anyone around him intelligent enough to hold his own in conversation, let alone be his friend, and who consequently spoke to pictures and statues of dead geniuses, Luthor was scrupulously sane. When he said he could navigate a distance of 26 light-years in a reasonable length of time, Superman was inclined to believe him.

On the trip to Metropolis Superman did Luthor the courtesy of wrapping him in his cape so that he didn't catch a worse cold than Superman had already furnished him. They could also make the trip faster that way. The cape protected Luthor from burning to a cinder with friction. They landed in the central courtyard of the Metro Modern Art Museum. The city was a ghost town early Sunday morning.

"Do you appreciate art, Noodles?" Luthor asked as he unraveled himself from the red cape.

"I think so. But my taste is a little more offbeat than these pieces."

There was a big round St. Bernard with the look of a monk standing by a fountain. It was carved from redwood. There was also an aluminum rectangular prism twelve feet long and bent in three places. Its title was "Crushed Cigarette." There were several stabiles, the most interesting of which was a silver-and-black structure made from several materials. In its center was an ovular plastic bulb whose top half was clear and whose bottom half was smoky black and opaque. It was surrounded by eight coiled flat silver surfaces, each maybe thirty feet long if it were unrolled. The sign accompanying the object called it "Black Widow" and noted that the piece was on indefinite loan from the artist, one Jeremy McAfee.

"There it is," Luthor swelled with unabashed pride, "my flying sailboat."

"What?"

"It's supposed to be lifted like a glider by a mother craft of some sort, but you'll serve the same purpose."

"You're telling me that this three-dimensional test pattern is your starship?"

"Well, you don't think it's art, do you? Just fly it up about twenty thousand feet and let go." Luthor pressed several unmarked points on the apparently smooth surface of the sculpture's central bulb, and the clear portion opened on a hinge like a cracked Easter egg.

As Luthor climbed inside, Superman became apprehensive. "What about McAfee? He's a very well-known artist."

"He's a sententious phony. If you like, I'll get a letter from him granting permission to use his sculpture for space flight as soon as we get back. The minute we touch down on Earth."

"Are you telling me that Jeremy McAfee is you?"

"I didn't say that."

"Who else are you?"

"Genghis Khan, Joan of Arc, Einstein. Do I ask you your secret identity? Everyone knows you're Morgan Edge, anyway."

Superman watched himself do a double take.

"Gotcha."

Superman lifted Luthor and his Black Widow four miles into the sky and let go. Majestically as a butterfly coming out of its cocoon the eight arms uncoiled as it fell. From each of their surfaces rose four triangular sails, black on one side and silver on the other, as if some old sea captain were pulling the strings all at once from outside the bottle. Everything but the pilot bubble was thinner than writing paper and as it fell, its speed approaching two hundred miles an hour, the silver sides of all thirty-two sails glowed with soaked up sunlight. Its descent slowed. Stopped. It rose. It gained speed. The arms and deceptively fragile sails railed against the rushing wind, but they held. And the wind diminished as the air thinned and the speed increased. By the time it crossed the edge of space the Black Widow flew faster than a comet. It streaked toward the sun.

Within half an hour Luthor was rolling in an arc around Sol, his ship itself glowing as brightly as a tiny white dwarf with a black egg at its core. It soaked energy from the star, whipped around it like an arm winding up to a pitch. It sprung out of orbit into the northern sky as fast as a photon. As it crossed the threshold of lightspeed it entered negative space. Lex Luthor had all time and space at his disposal. What was the difference, he wondered, between himself and a superman?

The last son of Krypton followed the sailing ship into the sky, fascinated as its sails swelled with solar energy and disappeared from real space. Superman followed under his own power. There was no way to say where in space he overtook Luthor, since neither was traveling in the visible Universe. They swam the catacombs of a thousand planes of existence and if during the trip they occasionally intersected with the three dimensions of their familiar perceptions it was by chance. As the first trickle of internal combustion engines began their inevitable Sunday flood over the streets of Metropolis, Superman dropped through the green skies of Oric.

20

The Arrivals

Clark Kent had seen this phenomenon on Earth once, when Robert Redford was starring in a movie being filmed in Metropolis for Galaxy Studios and the studio gave him an office in the Galaxy Building. Clark noticed Redford in the lobby buying a copy of the *Daily Planet*. Redford, nosing through the paper, didn't notice that although it was mid-morning when the lobby was generally empty, the population of the area where he was standing had increased several hundred percent since he walked in. During a period of nine minutes absolutely no one who walked by him either stepped out of the lobby or onto an elevator. Apparently Redford noticed none of this until a middle-aged woman walked up to the newsstand to buy a magazine, looked at him absently, and quite against her will she squealed. Redford looked around at the scores of people trying to be part of the décor, smiled nervously, and darted into the nearest elevator.

Similarly, Superman quickly decided that as long as he

was on Oric he should not stand still in any public place.

The world was a wasteland, mostly. Four-fifths of it was liquid, primarily water and ammonia, which was adequate for the gilled Lalofins from the Sirius system, but the sea did not even support life of its own any more, if it ever had. Most of the land was under a great equatorial glacial belt which grew and shrank only slightly as the seasons changed. Oric was tilted nearly 80 degrees to its orbit. There was only one collection of land masses on the planet in a region temperate enough so that hundreds of diverse races could adapt and function with relative equality. This region was on a tight group of islands referred to simply as the Archipelago, since it was the only archipelago on the planet and needed no more specific name.

The largest of the islands did have a name in most languages. The English equivalent was probably some variation of the word *cybernetic,* like Cybernia or Cyber Island. Cyber would have been an architect's nightmare and a technocrat's wet dream. Fortunately there was nowhere in the known Galaxy other than Earth where the craft of architecture was anyone's sole professional concern. There were lots of technocrats—as well as inventors, industrialists, engineers and salesmen—many of whom were considered successes in their field because they did most of their business here.

The island was tear-shaped, 78 kilometers long and 43 kilometers at its widest point. Presumably the ground under Cyber Island's city was mostly granules of silicon and green clay, as was the land surface left visible on the six other large islands in the Archipelago, as well as the scores of smaller ones. There was not a square centimeter of uncovered land anywhere on Cyber, and the paved surface extended several kilometers beyond the shore at all points in order to provide living and working facilities for creatures better adapted to liquid than gas respiration.

When Earthmen reached the stars—that time would be no longer than two generations, Superman knew—and moneymakers inevitably followed in the trail of the pioneers, this world of Oric would be a fine home away from home for them. In all his travels Superman had seen only one society more encumbered by rituals and traditions than the civilization of Oric, and that was Western society on Earth. The tradition and ritual here were a kind of artificial bond holding together an artificial society of disparate forms of life.

Most of the ritual, naturally, had to do with trade, which was the essential purpose of this society. Wandering over the byways of Cyber Island, leading a crowd of the curious, Superman paused to watch a merchant who apparently had just returned from the Spice Shower. This was a collection of meteoroids streaming through the void a little over a light-year from Sirius, which were rich in elements that could be refined into taste-enhancing food additives. These spices were very popular among bulk feeders like humanoids who had taste faculties.

Beings would pause at a small stand where the merchant displayed his wares and offer him elaborate gifts which the merchant traditionally refused. In return for the gracious offers, though, the merchant would insist that the beings taste his spices. When someone admired the taste of one or more of them at length the merchant would offer it as a gift, which the being would accept or decline. The being, if he accepted, would then offer his own gift in return and he and the merchant would dance around with various offers until they could agree upon an equitable exchange. At no time did either the buyer or seller actually say that one so-called gift was in payment for the other. It was all very amicable.

A crowd gathered like barnacles around Superman when he paused to offer the merchant a lump of coal from the pouch in his cape.

"Pardon me?" the merchant said.

"Coal. Carbon. You can write with it. You can burn it for a long time."

"How dense is it?"

Superman let the merchant weigh the object in his hand. He didn't seem impressed, but couldn't figure out how to tell the celebrity that this commodity was not even a suitable gift for a Pleiades microbe. The crowd murmured, or did something like murmuring.

"Oh, excuse me," Superman said with a smile, "but I don't suppose you'd want to burn it, anyway." He closed the lump in his two hands and squeezed. A tiny jet of black dust escaped through a crack between his two thumbs, but the last few specks of that dust seemed to twinkle before they hit the ground. He opened his hands and held a new object between thumb and forefinger. "Possibly you like it better in this form."

The merchant gaped for a moment, then fell back into his ritualized behavior as if he had not been caught by surprise. "I certainly could not accept such a gift from so august a personage as yourself, but for the gracious offer I insist you try my spices."

A single grain of each of a dozen spices touched to Superman's tongue was enough. He found the one he wanted. The merchant offered him about two grams of it in a sealed ceramic vial as Superman handed over the diamond that used to be a lump of coal. The crowd murmured again.

Apparently Superman gave the merchant the diamond too soon after the merchant gave him the spice. It seemed the merchant was offended.

"Oh, is that mine?" Superman tried to recover by handing back the little spice vial. "No, this is for a Terran friend. They have overly developed taste glands, you see. It is much too strong in this form. Keep the stone, of course, as a token of my esteem."

"Your esteem for me is its own reward. I need no token." He handed the Kryptonian the diamond and the onlookers seemed soothed. It worked.

"I can certainly see that the spice is diluted. Is ammonia the proper fluid for Earthlings?"

"Water would be better, but if you prefer to work with ammonia—"

"No, no, Superman sir. Water is no problem." The merchant riffled through the mess behind his stand and produced a beaker of water which he mixed with a small quantity of the spice and presented to Superman.

"Why, thank you," the hero paused a moment. "Tell me, might you have some use for a diamond stone?" He was starting to get the hang of it.

Superman estimated that he had a few hours to be visible on Oric before Luthor arrived and told someone in authority the story upon which they had agreed. The Kryptonian passed a small structure which was apparently a real estate office where a machine-like being was describing subdivisions of a completely inorganic satellite circling a planet in the Outer Darkness region of the Polaris system. Odd, Superman thought. He did not recall that particular planet's having a moon.

Several kilometers to the west, on the Master's island, an outlandish, bulbous craft made a landing on the truncated tip of the pryamid and sat there like an egg in a cup. The Master immediately had his associates disable and investigate the vehicle.

21

The Interrogation

Luthor remembered nothing that had happened since he turned the dial to roll in the eighth arm of his Black Widow. He needed a fairly stable place to set down the rounded bottom of his bulb, and the obvious site was the slightly truncated tip of this pyramid. He congratulated himself on both his successful touchdown and its spectacular nature. He was still congratulating himself when he found himself prone on a flat surface, waking up, completely unclothed.

The floor was a kind of plastic, or maybe some sort of porous concrete. It was about as hard as the floor of a gymnasium. The room was blue and had twelve equal walls as well as a thirteenth about twice the width of each of the other twelve. Each had a disc on it; the one on the thirteenth wall was larger and blank. Luthor at first thought the other twelve were pictures of some sort. Pictures of the faces of different unfamiliar aliens. The faces seemed to be pictures until one, with mandibles and antennae like a giant green cockroach, wiggled its left feeler and moved its mouth and a sound came out.

"The subject appears conscious," the roach said.

Luthor heard the words in a kind of squeaky, chirpy voice. The kind of voice one would expect from an anthropomorphic insect.

There was a blue glow in the room. Even Luthor's skin appeared to have a blue tint. There was a round object hanging from the peaked ceiling about thirty feet over Luthor's head as he stood, but it didn't seem to be the light source. Maybe it was the loudspeaker. The light seemed to come from the walls themselves. The bug's face appeared on the big round screen on the largest of the thirteen walls.

"Identify yourself, humanoid," the grotesque face demanded.

"Where am I? Am I inside the pyramid? Am I still on Oric?" Even naked and imprisoned, Luthor was not to be dominated. He was used to incarceration and the attention it brought.

"You will answer these inquiries. Are you Luthor the Earthling technician?"

"I prefer the term Terran, actually. Earthling always sounded kind of sappy to me."

"Non sequitur. Are Earthlings not Earthlings?"

The insect was replaced on the large screen by another of the faces from around the wall. This one was a yellow-skinned character with scales and a beak for a mouth. Luthor recognized it as a native of the Polaris group. "I believe the subject does not realize he is hearing the intentional translator over his head. When any of us refers to your racial ancestry it is translated in your perception into whatever word you expect to hear."

"You mean I hear you saying Earthling but if I wanted to I could hear you say Terran?"

"Non sequitur," the bug-thing said again.

"I know, I know. They sound like the same word to you." Luthor was very pleased. He'd learned something new. "What's my race now, bug-eyes?"

"As I referred to you before, you are a Terran. I am a bug-head. The creature who just addressed you is a vulture-face. We will ask all further questions."

Luthor wondered if any of his interrogators could fathom the reason for his wide grin, or if they knew what a grin was. Here he was, twenty-six light-years from home, locked in some crazy room in his birthday suit listening to his jailers insult themselves. He hadn't enjoyed being locked up this much in years.

"Please attend, humanoid," the beak-nosed being came back to the main screen. "Are you the Terran scientist Luthor?"

"Yes. Yes I am, worm-digger. You must've seen the label inside my prison fatigues, right?"

A crystalline creature, like a huge diamond whose only asymmetric feature was a belt around its apparent waist, came on the screen. "What is the nature of your vehicle?"

"My vehicle? Oh, the one you took away from me along with my clothes. Hope you know enough not to send the sails to the laundry with the fatigues. The cruiser is a highly efficient solar energy absorber. It soaks up power from the stars much in the way a sailboat catches the wind, only my craft has the capability of storing massive quantities of energy like a battery for use in propelling it through planes of existence where starlight may not be available."

There was a pause in the questioning.

Presently another questioner came on the screen, a flat-faced nearly humanoid being with teeth and whiskers like a rat and a nose below its mouth. "How is it a creature from a society as technologically underdeveloped as your own is capable of designing a craft more efficient than those in use on Oric?"

"Technology has nothing to do with it. The principles of solar energy are very simple. The only problem was in coming up with a new way to use them. I chose to merge the idea of a sailboat with the use of power from the stars rather than from the winds. I am very good at that sort of reasoning, if I may say so."

"Why did you choose Oric as your destination?"

"Well, it wouldn't prove anything about interstellar navigation if I went to Poughkeepsie, would it?"

"Non sequitur."

"No sense of humor at all. You remind me of this guy I know who flies around in his underwear. Look, to tell you the truth, I came because of this character Towbee who turned up on Earth a few days ago."

Another pause in the questioning. This time all the screens went blank, and when they lit up again there was a new questioner on the big wall. Luthor had no idea what part of this being was its face, if it had a face. It looked a lot like a cross between a record turntable and an electric broom.

"How is it that the minstrel inspired your visit to this world?" the spinning vacuum cleaner asked through the translator.

"He sang some nonsensical song about the coming of some big honcho who'd rule this arm of the Galaxy when certain things happened. I looked at a map of the Galaxy and figured it was this arm, because there's no other promontory of the Galaxy that looks like an arm. He said this guy was a hybrid from Vega and when I got here this was the only planet that seemed capable of supporting complex forms of life, hybrid or otherwise. Something in the song about sailing ships used for starflight made me think of the thing I flew here in. I wanted to get in on the action, that's all. Earth's a bust, you may have heard."

There was yet another pause in the questioning, although this one was different. For a moment Luthor sensed a new quality in the manners of his questioners, as if the very texture of the air in the room were changing. Then he fell unconscious.

The image on the big screen rippled into the face of the Master. He conferred with his twelve slaves.

Luthor wondered why he was suddenly lying on the floor again. Then he realized he had probably been put to sleep again for at least a few moments. He wasn't angry about this, it was part of the game he was playing. Vulture-beak addressed him.

"The Master would have you enter his service. He frankly has doubts about your sincerity which he would like allayed. Have you any information or commodity for the Master who has made you a gift of the privilege of his service?

"He wants me to go to work for him and he wants me to give him something? He ought to give me something—like maybe retirement benefits at least."

"Non sequitur."

"When I give him something, it's a privilege; when he gives me something it's a non sequitur. I get it."

"The Terran is approaching arrogance." Luthor had wondered how long it would take them to notice.

"Look, how would the Master like Superman? Does he qualify as a commodity?"

Another pause. A longer one this time.

The diamond creature was back on the big screen. "The humanoid Superman is reportedly on Oric at this moment, although his reasons for visiting are unknown. How can you furnish the Master with Superman?"

"He's here? Ahead of me. Wish I knew how he knew I'd be headed here. But I do know one thing, and that's that I know him as well as he knows me. I know how he'll react to just about anything that falls his way. Just do what I say. I'll need the help of about four of you, and freedom to wander around the civilized parts of this planet, of course. And I won't be doing it just for this Master of yours. That bone-brained muscleman's tracked me down everywhere on Earth already. Now he's followed me here. If this Master wants Superman he can have him, but it'll be my score I'll be evening up."

All thirteen screens went blank for Luthor didn't know how long. Solitary confinement on Earth was nothing like being alone even for moments trillions of miles from home. But his would-be tormentors who were his companions were back again, the broom speaking.

"The Master has directed us to act according to your specifications," it said.

22

The Hotel

There was something like a hotel on Cyber Island. It was like a hotel, but it was more like some sort of a referral agency. Scattered around the island were buildings and houses and caves and tanks full of various combinations of liquids and gases which were available, in return for appropriate gifts to the management of the hotel, for temporary habitation by different races with different creature needs. The hotel consisted of a single office inhabited by individuals of various races in various miniature environments.

A recent customer of the hotel was referred to a small three-room suite at the southern tip of Cyber overlooking the water and ammonia sea. The suite was specially equipped with a twenty percent oxygen atmosphere and a deodorizer which substituted a scent of the humanoid occupant's choice—a smell something like that of a wine cellar whose kegs and bottles had overflowed years ago, drowning several hundred rats, but there wasn't a lot to choose from, and it was better than the alternatives—for the normal external environment. The humanoid was registered at the hotel under the name Abraham Lincoln.

"I would like to examine the register for the past day," the rich voice filtered through the intentional translator that hung around the neck of the attendant at one console of the hotel.

"I'll take care of you in a moment," Superman heard the attendant say. The little six-armed, four-legged creature faced the wall pressing buttons and turning dials and scratching notations and punching holes at certain places in a plasticine tape running by his waist to his heart's content. Superman checked and found that the creature did indeed have a heart.

The attendant was a native of Rigel-9, as were about a third of the hotel's employees. The Rigellian had almost no reasoning capacity beyond that which was necessary to repeat something he had heard or copy down something he had seen. The size of the Rigellian's brain, however, was comparable with that of a human and until he approached senility, which was usually around 120 or so, he could remember the events immediately following his birth with the clarity of the present. Even the Guardians did not bother to keep an updated record of the race's history. The Rigellians used the surface area of the thirty-six largely worthless planets and satellites other than Rigel-9, which circled their star, for the purpose of storing the records of everything that happened to every Rigellian for the past seven million years. They were born to be clerical workers.

Superman did not particularly impress the Rigellian clerk, although it would probably be important for the Rigellian to record the celebrity's actions in his personal record. "I am ready now, Superman. What is it you want to know?"

"I am looking for a human who may have registered here recently. Would you remember if you saw him?"

"Of course I would remember. During what period of time do you estimate that this being appeared here?"

Superman indicated the Orician equivalent of twenty-four hours and gave the creature a physical description of Luthor. Nothing of that nature, according to the clerk, had been to the hotel recently. But Earthmen, with their filtrums, were fairly conspicuous here. Was it possible he was disguised? Perhaps, the Kryptonian asked, he could see the record of who had been in and out in the past day?

"Of course," the Rigellian obliged. "Name: Cephula-332. Point of origin: Sirius-4. Name: Zoorpng. Point of origin: Delphinius-1. Name—"

"Excuse me. Hold on. Wait a minute."

"Did you get the information you wanted?"

"No, not actually. Maybe if I looked over your records myself."

"We are quite efficient. We do what we do better than anyone else in the Galaxy," the Rigellian insisted. "Perhaps you want only the names. Cephula-332; Zoorpng; The Draxyl Mount; Malthusan—"

"I'm sure you are very good at what you do." Superman smiled instinctively, although its meaning probably

164

did not come across. "But what you do is not what I'm after right now."

"Do you want information?"

"Yes, I do."

"We are the most efficient repositories of information in the known Galaxy, I assure you." Superman did not care to devise a trick of logic to get at what passed in the Rigellian for a mind. "I am sure you will find what you want here. Cephula-332; Zoorpng; The Draxyl Mount; Malthusan; Seventh Horg . . ."

The wall console that the clerk manipulated was a little like a computer terminal, a little like a golf course. As Superman scanned its memory nodes with x-ray vision he was thankful that he did not have the opportunity to tamper with it physically. It had all sorts of sand traps into which an unwary alien might fall. For example, if he had been given access to the records, he now found as he scanned it and ignored the Rigellian's discourse, the first thing he would have done was apply body heat to certain sensors on the console and speak a command into a speaker of some sort behind the Rigellian. If he had done that—a perfectly logical action from the point of view of an Earthman after a cursory examination of the mechanism—the machine would have sent an impulse to the other consoles in the room and they would all have immediately begun spewing ammonia bubbles from their feed-out orifices. The mechanisms were simple recording devices and were not dangerous per se. They were dangerous only the way a telephone might be dangerous if there were an alien around whose natural response to the ringing of such a device might be to throw it into a filled bathtub and unwittingly electrocute the tub's occupant.

"Olin-Sang 2." The idiot savant clerk droned the colorfully bizarre names of the heterogeneous group of beings who had availed themselves of the hotel's services that day. "Gerstenzang Gryzmish; Squire Onorato Sgan; Cholmondeley . . ."

But now the Kryptonian had it licked. There was what appeared to be a chronological list of the hotel's recent patrons, scattered across the machine's memory in a pattern that at first looked random, then made sense only if one started to understand it by dismissing all Earth-born concepts of sequences and if-then relationships and the things that are taught in logic courses.

"Full Hand Band," the Rigellian continued. "Scorpio Bearing 32 Degrees Sirius (That was somebody's name, based on the position in space of the cargo ship where he was born); Ptang-Ptang Click . . ."

There it was. Superman didn't stop to figure out the odds for some extraterrestrial creature's being named Abraham Lincoln. Luthor was a clever fellow; Superman was glad to have him on his side this time around. The scientist was playing on his own well-established weaknesses. He was playing the role of a person on the run who needed to assume an alias and who could not resist the joke on a world where no one could possibly recognize the name, of taking a very famous name from Earth. But in doing that, Luthor gave his new-found ally a signal of his whereabouts that did not have to be prearranged.

Superman would go to this suite at the southern end of Cyber Island where this Abraham Lincoln was registered and he would find Luthor there. Luthor would make a convincing show of hostility, Superman would pretend to be caught short by whatever gadget Luthor used on him, and together the hero and the scientist would be taken into the Master's complex as captive and captor. Superman stopped the Rigellian clerk's catechism and thanked him with the gift of a lump of coal the Kryptonian pulled from the pouch in his cape where he kept his Clark Kent clothes compressed into little wafers. He squeezed the coal in his hand and put it under enough pressure to turn it into carbon's purest state, that of a raw diamond.

The costumed humanoid strode smiling back to the entrance of the big referral office. At the entrance he leaped up at the sky, through a ring of red light that surrounded the doorway like a globe. The light caught him like a bug in a spiderweb.

He should have noticed it. He would have seen it on Earth, but his perceptions were off. Colors and shapes under the blue star Vega were not quite what they were on Earth, and Superman's visual perceptions were weakened, anyway. Somehow, from somewhere, a mesh of filtered light was beamed across his path and he was caught in light of the frequency generated by a red star —the kind Krypton orbited—the kind that left him without super powers. They were slipping away.

The last thing Superman saw was the ground, where Luthor stood surrounded by a group of four creatures of different races. Each raised a gun-like device of Luthor's design and squeezed back on the trigger.

And the last thing Superman heard himself saying was, "Stupid! *Stupid! STUPID!*"

23

The Secret

The Tripedal at the entrance to the decontamination chamber was a pushover. All Luthor needed to cajole him into giving passage was a good word and one of the diamonds Luthor found in Superman's cape pouch when they brought the Kryptonian down outside the hotel. Substances of dense matter were, as a rule, considered valuable on Oric. In the pouch Luthor also found some colorful trinkets in the shape of wafers. They were apparently some compressed material placed there for safekeeping, some sort of woven plastic, maybe. Luthor had no time to analyze the wafers chemically, and he did not even stop to wonder what Superman would want with the pair of eyeglasses he found there also.

Luthor had no time to worry about that sort of trivia now; he was too busy being horrified. There was an urgent matter to take care of, and Superman, unconscious in the interrogation room beyond the decontamination chamber, was the only hope for a solution.

The past three days for Luthor were among the finest he could remember, and he had no scruples about letting his old enemy spend some time getting his mind homogenized by the Master and his merry men. Luthor was doing what he did best: science with undercurrents of intrigue. At this point the Master claimed to trust Luthor, but still had not shown the Earthman his face. It was probably grotesque. The Master was reputedly a hybrid of more races than anyone had ever accurately determined. It was the boss's slaves who stashed Luthor in a room outfitted to his specifications with a blackboard, a desk, a drawing board, a robot calculator that followed him through the halls as he paced and was activated by voice commands, a big garbage can, and reams of paper for filling it up. Also, Luthor now wore a copy of his purple-and-green flying suit, complete with all sorts of neat gadgets for blasting through walls, delivering electric shocks, injecting deadly serums, and that sort of thing. Luthor never ever, not even once, told anyone the fact that he took secret delight in the fact that he was born under the sign of Scorpio.

A written memorandum from the Master himself gave Luthor the problem he was to solve. He had to calculate from gravitational data the number of black holes along the inner border of the Galactic Arm, as well as each hole's size and mass. It was a delicious game of mathematical cat-and-mouse. And so as not to get bored with momentarily insoluble questions, Luthor spent spare moments collecting data from his robot computer about the Master's base of operations here with an eye to getting clues as to the whereabouts of the Einstein document.

Here was how the Galaxy was held together:

All matter was effectively the same. Matter's basic elements were protons, electrons, neutrons, and such smaller particles as helped certain atoms and molecules to specialize. Even among the specialized atoms and molecules, the major function of all matter was to expend energy. Most of the energy expended by matter was a cohesive force called gravitation. It was gravitation that not only held the molecules of planet-bound objects together and attracted objects to planets and stars in a very orderly fashion, but gravitational energy also held planets and other bodies in orbit around stars and held stars fairly close to each other so that there was a well-defined Galaxy. Stars attracted each other with gravitation and stuck together in their various orbits. But with simple computation it became clear that there was not enough matter in all the stars and planets to attract bodies across expanses of light-years and hold something as big as the Galaxy together. The visible heavenly bodies, in fact, provided only about half the cohesive force necessary to hold the Galaxy together. The rest was provided by black holes.

Black holes were bodies of very heavy matter that once were stars. Young stars, like Earth's yellow sun, burned themselves up with reckless enthusiasm for tens of millions of years. Old stars, like Krypton's giant red sun Antares, were no more than amorphous masses of gas and vapor without anything that could be called a solid surface, but which were so large that once they burned themselves down and the stuff that made them up fell cold toward the core of the dying star, the particles of mass exerted so much gravitational force on one another that their very molecules intersected. The resulting object, the dead husk of a once flaming star, was a black hole, an object ranging in size from several cubic centimeters to a few thousand miles in diameter, and so dense that even pure energy could not escape its gravitational force. What little starlight they still generated never got off the surface. The black holes were the glue of the Galaxy.

As Luthor played hide-and-seek with the black holes over the expanse of space that separated the Arm in which Vega and Sol burned from the rest of the Guardians' sphere of influence, that silly little doggerel of the space minstrel played handball off the back wall of his mind:

When the minions of immortals spread Galactic,
When a thousand cultures dwell in Vega's glow,
When a sailing ship for starflight is a tactic,
When these things all come to pass then we will know

That a hybrid born to Vega has been spreading
Massive strength through an empire built on trade,
And a path to an Arm's rule he is treading;
'Gainst his rule need for freedom sure will fade.

Luthor asked his computer friend—he had named the machine MacDuff—how many distinct races, at the last count, frequented the markets of Oric. The answer was 997. From what he could decipher from data he coaxed out of the computer he could see that the Master's biggest concern was real estate. He apparently specialized in subdividing the surfaces of totally dead planets and setting up communities dependent on his shipping and teleportation operations for their life support. Luthor could actually coax a lot of information out of MacDuff using various computer codes he figured out. Most of what he got, though, seemed to be gibberish. Somebody would understand it. Superman probably would, he grudgingly admitted, but not because he was any great intellect. His intelligence was above average, and that along with total recall would make it possible for Superman to explain the meanings of all these alien symbols which certainly held the answer to the location of the Einstein document. But locating either the document or Superman seemed a problem of great difficulty.

The scientist wondered, not a lot, because he was enjoying the other complex matters on his mind, exactly why this character with designs on the rule of an entire sector of the Galaxy was interested in the location of black holes. Industrialists, politicians, bureaucrats, Luthor knew a lot of them and this faceless Master was all those things. People like that were so concerned with the trappings and textures of the empires they sought to build that they wasted valuable commodities like Luthor's intellect on self-indulgent matters like mapmaking. That was certainly the only reason the Master was so inordinately concerned with the uncharted black holes that were sprinkled over his prospective kingdom.

Luthor dismissed the Master as the latest in a long line of false Messiahs who ached to make an ancient prophesy come true about himself.

Here was something interesting, Luthor thought, as he pulled a plasticine tape from a feed slot on MacDuff. If his previous assumptions about the mathematical codes used in the Master's computer indexes were correct, then this piece of read-out had something to do with time travel. No, not time travel. Actual mass shipments of materials through time. What was this character planning? An import and export business with the Stone Age?

Luthor put the read-out on a growing pile of alien computer gibberish he was collecting in a corner of the room and sat down at his drawing board.

"MacDuff," Luthor addressed the machine, which responded by lighting a red signal on its front plate, "get me a three-dimensional projection of the planetary system of the star Delphinus immediately preceding the time it became a nova."

The robot wheeled out of the room. Luthor fiddled with his adjustable protractor trying to triangulate the location of a massive invisible body somewhere between Delphinus and a star yet undiscovered by Earth astronomers which Luthor named after himself. He looked up in the middle of ruling a straight line and his mouth fell open.

Nine hundred ninety-seven races, he thought. Sailing ship, he thought. Time shipments? Real estate? Black holes?

Somewhere Luthor had heard, or he had read, or he had reasoned, that the Guardians didn't consider wandering stars within their jurisdiction. They considered them outside the Galaxy because they did not orbit the Central Cluster as did the other stars. Wandering stars were just passing through, not held to the main body of the Galaxy by attraction to black holes or other stars' gravitation. The immortals apparently felt that anything not part of the actual Milky Way unit by permanent attraction was outside their concern.

Could it be that the Master had a practical concern with the location of the black holes Luthor was charting? He ran down the hall after the robot MacDuff, knocking down or pushing out of the way six or eight creatures from as many worlds who were the Master's slaves, or employees, or elves, or whatever they called them here.

"MacDuff!"

The robot stopped and spun around, flashing its red signal.

"Get back to my office. The request for the data on Delphinus is countermanded."

Luthor spent the night with no more thoughts of locating black holes. He had to decode as much information as MacDuff could intercept from other computer units with regard to Superman. Where was he? In what kind of condition? Has he ever been conscious at all since his capture? Maybe if Luthor could find the document, he could find Superman.

Luthor had dealt with the Central Intelligence Agency, the Federal Bureau of Investigation, the Soviet KGB, and a score of other monomaniacal institutions across the Earth that had made a religion out of secrecy. The Master was a little-leaguer by comparison.

After several hours of feverish button-pushing, nonsense code-word repetition, and mathematical calculation Luthor learned that the Einstein document was in the interrogation chamber one level below the base of the pyramid. After a few minutes he was able to ask the robot what was in that decontamination chamber. As Luthor expected, the answer to that query decoded into the word "Superman."

Luthor established that the entrance to the room was guarded by a single Tripedal, so as to allay any suspicions by those who should not have any suspicions. Luthor obtained a psychological profile, such as it was, of the dull-witted guard. He also requested an account of Superman's physical condition. A combination of drugs and a bombardment of external sensory stimuli put the hero into a suggestible state. For about an hour each day he was left alone and dazed so that he didn't regress into permanent catatonia and become useless to the Master.

Luthor requested a series of chemicals from MacDuff. For safety's sake, he told the robot that he wanted them to mix a superior type of ink. It was true that the blue soup with which the Master provided him ran all over the paper and Luthor could not abide sloppy calculations.

A few minutes into the hour that was to precede Superman's fifth day of interrogation Luthor entered the interrogation room. He found his old enemy lying across a slab of what, on Oric, had to be a terribly expensive chunk of hard rock, his head propped up on a silvery pillow you could get lost in. If Michelangelo were here to see the massive alien lying helpless and motionless as a statue, he would drool with envy at the work of a superior hand.

Luthor tried to pick Superman's head up but a touch of the pillow gave him an unexpected electrical shock. He couldn't hold the Kryptonian's head up by the wiry hair, for he would end up with slashes all over his hand. He ended by clutching the terribly potent chemical mixture gingerly between two fingers as he pried the hero's jaws open with both hands. For the first time Luthor was glad that hard labor in prison had kept his arms in shape.

Luthor dumped most of the liquid between the deadly rows of bleach-white teeth before they snapped shut. He pounded and pressed on the man's throat until he could feel the mixture of antitoxins and amino acids passing by. This might bring him around; it would probably kill him.

24

The Mad Dream

This was the day Superman was introduced to God.

He was asleep. Dreaming. Dreaming dreams somebody else wanted him to dream. Dreams about a language he was practically born speaking and whose written form was poured into his mind one day in his infancy and which his young mind gulped down like mother's milk. Dreams about his mother Lara and his father Jor-El. He rarely dreamed about them any more. And a dream about a pair of quatrains that sang themselves repeatedly at him, quatrains, he somehow knew, that were first written by Sonnabend the lawgiver:

> Star Child will leave a deathworld
> For the System of the Rings,
> Where the child will grow to legend
> As his life the singer sings.
>
> When the conqueror wants his secret
> With the Star Child he'll contend;
> And when day of battle's over
> Then the legend's life will end.

Star Child. In Kryptonese that was Kal-El. He was Kal-El. He'd told somebody that. In his dream. Or did he say it out loud while he was dreaming? In any case, it made somebody happy. Superman liked to make people happy.

Usually.

Was it for days he dreamed? Minutes? Centuries? Who knew? There was something unusual about these dreams. There were more words in them than pictures. Kryptonese words.

He dreamed until a lump of liquid appeared in his mouth, and he felt, in his sleep, half the lump dribble down his chin and the rest pour into his body.

He knew every cubic centimeter of his body, inside and out. He could check out his pancreas by simply looking at it. But he couldn't do that in his dream. The liquid compound slid down his esophagus, through his digestive system, seeped out the walls of his intestines, decomposed into single huge molecules and a single molecule grabbed at each cell in his body; they fanned in all directions to his toes, to the follicles of his steel-hard hair. It made him high. Higher than flying. Higher than the time barrier.

This compound, or mixture, or nightmare, was doing

176

something to him he couldn't control. Something nothing had ever done before. The dreams were gone, the feelings were gone, the powers were gone.

He was dying.

When the dreams about words were gone he was somewhere new, and maybe someone new, and he was being propelled through time and space and something besides time and space by a power that certainly was not his own, into a tiny white light at infinity. The light grew and became something more than white, more than colors. There were colors that even Superman, with his heightened perceptions, had never before been capable of seeing. But he could see now that this thing he was approaching was a kind of grid with crosspieces of all colors against which there tumbled thousands, millions, trillions of beings of nearly as many races and conditions. Each one—each creature, flared into a rainbow explosion as it hit the grid and vanished. And that was where Superman was going.

He recognized some of the races of these beings. A humanoid here and there. Some Rannians, Arachnoids, Chloroplads. He could not watch them quickly enough. He felt he had to stop moving, to stand still, to go the other way. When the grid tumbled up into his face . . .

. . . and the Universe turned white.

"Kal-El."

The voice was very close.

"Kal-El, you are all right."

There seemed to be a face and a form that went with this voice. A very friendly feeling as well.

"Kal-El, please. We have a great deal to do, and I believe you have a decision to make."

"Who?" Superman asked approximately.

"I am an old friend." It was a man, an Earthman, also approximately. "We have very little time for the protocol to which everyone else coming here is entitled. I hope you will not require that sort of nonsense; you have always

177

seemed most capable of acclimating to new conditions fairly quickly."

It was an old man. A man who seemed always to have been old. With a furry white head of hair and a mustache. His face was an infinity of wrinkles holding a corncob pipe.

"Pardon my simplicity," Superman said, "but have I by any chance died?"

"Possibly," the old man said. "That is not for me to explain. I am an intermediary. My job is to see that the transition from your previous plane of existence to this one is smooth, although in your case there are extenuating circumstances."

"Please," Superman said, "I'm very confused. Tell me what's happened to me and what happens next."

"You have about deduced what has happened to you. Next you are to meet your Creator."

"My—"

"It is not common procedure, of course."

"God?"

"You are better at words than I am, Kal-El. It is I who am supposed to come to the point, and you seem to beat me there. Yes, God."

"There is a tradition, sir, in every religious culture I have ever encountered, which holds that anyone who looks upon the face of God will certainly die."

"We have all seen the face of God, as well as that of His Adversary whom He created. We are born with both in our hearts because they live in our souls forever."

"Thank you." Superman believed he was smiling.

"For what, Kal-El?"

"Your last couple of sentences very simply answered a handful of basic questions that tend to perplex us mortals through our whole lives."

"Do not make the assumption that you can group yourself among mortals, Kal-El. Not yet."

Superman could have no idea what the old man meant by that, but he was getting used to the idea of meeting God. He didn't want to spend much more time thinking about that before it happened. It would likely drive him mad.

It seemed probable to Superman that this particular event was at least as significant as stories of visions and prophesies and such as they were recorded in sacred writings of the various religions. He often wondered if the people in those stories were as forthright and no-nonsense in their dealings with one another as the writings made them out to be.

In the Bible, for example, nobody messed around. If somebody wanted to say something to someone, he said it. There were no arguments. If somebody disagreed, there was a big fight, no preliminaries to waste time. No wonder those people lived so long. But here Superman was, on the threshold of Eternity, with enough questions to fill up most of that time in the asking.

"Why are you here to meet me? Have I met you?"

"We have several friends in common."

"Luthor?"

"In a way. I was thinking, actually, of Police Chief Parker, your foster parents the Kents, and your natural father Jor-El."

There was another thing that never seemed to happen in Bible stories: somebody was confused by something someone else said. "Huh?" Superman asked.

"Kal-El, it is time," the old man said. "Prepare to meet your Creator."

Superman felt weak as the white turned whiter. He felt his mind blending with his body and his soul growing to the size of the Universe and his consciousness becoming aware of everything that he ever was and a head glowing with something more than light filled his sight and spoke:

—I am the Lord—

It was the face of Jor-El he saw.

—More than any other of My creations in your Galaxy you, the man called Star Child, are able to determine your own destiny—

"My destiny? What is my destiny?"

—If you had only one destiny I would not have given you powers and abilities far beyond those of mortal men . . . your destiny and that of your Galaxy, indeed, the destiny of all you touch, are one—

"Doesn't everyone determine his own destiny?"

—An electron that is part of an atom in an ocean may determine on which energy level it orbits, but it does not affect the coming and going of the tides . . . a man may decide when to sleep and eat, but not when to be born or die, or when his star sun goes nova . . . only you have such a choice—

"The choice of when to die?"

—The choice of whether to die—

Superman stared into the face of his father.

—If you choose to die, the Galaxy will certainly follow its appointed course which I illuminated to the one called Sonnabend these ages past . . . if you choose to continue, your future is your own . . . you may defeat the plans of him who plots to divide your Galaxy, or you may fall at his hands . . . whatever you choose, your reward will be the same . . . you have nothing to gain, in Earth or Heaven or Eternity, by opposing the inexorable flow of history, save the peace and freedom of your fellow beings . . . you are as a wild card in the scheme of Creation . . . there have been few I have sent to your Galaxy whose power of destiny was as great as your own—

Superman did not notice the apparent unseemliness of the wild card analogy coming from that Source until later. Now the only thing he was capable of noticing was the intent and the significance of it all. "Tell me, please," he asked, "who was the last one like me?"

—There have been many who chose to maintain neutrality when the choice came to them, many of whom you have never heard . . . one, however, was the one called the lawgiver, Sonnabend . . . the time is come . . . choose—

Superman decided whether to live or die.

"Coming around?" were the words the hero heard.

"Where am I?"

"Somewhere in the pyramid, imprisoned." Luthor's hands were beet red from slapping the Kryptonian's steely face. It was a dumb thing to do, but he had to do something with his hands.

"Daddy?" Superman asked.

"Come on. You're fighting it," the voice said. "It nearly got you for a moment, but you're fighting it."

Superman was coming back to his body again. He felt the familiar organs of his chest and stomach appearing back where they belonged, the dark viscous blood coursing through his arteries faster than a speeding bullet. It was Luthor's voice he was hearing now, rooting for him, urging him back to the world of three dimensions and energy-matter relationships, where there was a good and an evil and where the distinction was not very difficult to make.

"I saved you!" Luthor grabbed his sometime enemy's shoulders, jumping up and down. "I don't believe it. I saved your life!"

"No, you didn't." Superman smiled. "I think you finally managed to kill me."

25

The Atrocity

"Listen," Luthor said. "Listen, this is important."

"What?"

"I found out the Master's racket. I don't think even the Guardians know this plan, and it's reprehensible."

"Reprehensible? For a guy who once posed as a Korean guru just to attract 33 thousand impressionable teenage kids to a rally in Metro Stadium and hold them for ransom, he must be going some for you to call him reprehensible."

"I nearly went broke that year. Besides, you'd be surprised at how many followers I still have. What this clown's doing is worse. Much worse."

"Yeah?"

"Tell me, Muscles, how far does the Guardians' jurisdiction extend?"

"To the Areas of Dominant Gravitation of all stars and black holes in the Milky Way Galaxy."

"And when's a star considered to be in the Milky Way Galaxy, according to that definition?"

"That's any star subject to the cohesive forces that make the Galaxy a definable physical unit. Is this a social studies test? I thought you had some kind of secret to tell me."

"I do. What about wandering stars? The rogue stars that are just passing through along the edges of the Galaxy. What power do the Guardians have over them?"

"They have absolute power; physically, they're pretty much the most powerful creatures ever known. But they're morally banned from extending their powers to certain areas and they can only interfere with rogue stars if they somehow jeopardize the rest of the Galaxy—if they're about to incinerate an inhabited world or something. It's one of the laws that goes back to the Guardians' founding, apparently to make sure they didn't become absolute rulers of the Galaxy."

"Okay, now tell me the verse that lunatic singer Towbee quoted from this Sonnabend's prophesies, the one about what would happen before this Czar of the Galactic Arm would emerge? What was it? You've got total recall."

"When the minions of immortals spread Galactic,
When a thousand cultures dwell in Vega's glow,
When a sailing ship for starflight is a tactic,
When these things all—"

"That's enough. The immortals' minions, they're the Green Lanterns. Are they all over the Galaxy? Is there any place that isn't covered by them?"

"No. They're in every sector, have been for about four thousand years."

"And the sailing ship for starflight. I brought that here. The Black Widow, right?"

"That would probably qualify."

"And a thousand cultures. Could Sonnabend have been estimating? Would he possibly have meant, say, 997 races living here?"

"No. I understand he is quite precise. A thousand only turns out to be a round number in our decimal system."

"Whew, then we've got time. According to the portable computer terminal the Master's stooges issued me, there are 997 distinct races as of the last census. We've come here so that makes 998."

"I'm a Kryptonian, remember, not an Earthman."

"Oh, right. Well, that only makes 999."

"The Old-Timer. The defrocked Guardian," Superman said. "He told me he was the first Guardian to leave Oa. He was here. He makes a thousand."

"Bingo. There isn't a moment to lose. Listen, you know how the Master made his real estate killing?"

"On an offhand, guess, I'd say he cheated."

"You bet he cheated. He ripped off this Delphinian scientist's prototype time-snatcher. He's got this machine that can reach into the past or the future and pull inorganic matter into the present or place things in another time. He built a time-snatcher powerful enough to manufacture duplicate planets."

"You're telling me he buys a planet—"

"Buying things is taboo here. They exchange gifts."

"And he reaches, say, a hundred years or so into the future and brings back the planet from there so he's got two of them to sell?"

"Or three or a dozen or a hundred. And he goes and sells them all as if they were real planets—completely lifeless and good for nothing but housing developments —when all but one will disappear a hundred or so years later, leaving the inhabitants floating in empty space."

"That'll upset the whole space-time continuum for light-years around. It'll kill billions. He's mad."

"That makes him nothing worse than a dishonest businessman—like those guys that sell land in the Poconos, only on a bigger scale. He had me in this back room here figuring out where all the black holes are on the border between the Galactic Arm and the main body of the Galaxy."

"What's that got to do with it?"

"He's got the capability to grab every black hole on that border and throw it a billion years into the future. He's planning on dismembering the Arm from the rest of the Galaxy. The Guardians will be powerless to stop him from taking a conquering horde across every star system that rejects his tyrannical rule. The old guys will even be obligated to disarm the Green Lanterns already here. The Arm won't go anywhere right away, but it'll no longer be physically a part of the Galaxy. In a billion years it'll be spinning off, a mini-Galaxy of its own, but before that all Hell will break lose with the Master playing Satan."

"Oh, my God."

26

Collate

In the secretarial pool on the eighth floor of the Galaxy Building was a rather amazing machine built and leased to Galaxy Communications by the Xerox Corporation. The function of this machine was simply to reproduce what was written on paper. That is, if a sheet of paper with something written on it were slid into a certain slot of the machine, the images on that paper would have a bright light shined on them and then the images would be momentarily recorded inside the machine. The machine would then grab the top sheet of blank paper from a pile of its own supply, print the information in total from the first sheet on this second sheet of paper, belch the new copy out into a neat little pile of such copies, and immediately forget the information it had just recorded, ready to copy a fresh sheetful. To the machine, of course, this information it recorded and copied was not writing or drawing or anything meaningful at all. It was gibberish. Lines, points, curves, and such had no significance to the machine. The machine did nothing to the information, it simply recorded this for the benefit of the machine's operator, exactly as it appeared on the original copy.

Xerox Corporation did not sell these machines, or any of the many similar models which they manufactured. This equipment was only leased, and the corporation kept scrupulous track of their products. Occasionally certain illegal and morally questionable things were done with these remarkable machines. For example, Earth people would use a Xerox copier to reproduce several copies— in effect, to publish—written material legally protected from such free publication by unenforceable copyright laws. Another problem with Xerox copiers was that they disappeared with alarming frequency. They mysteriously vanished, from time to time, from the offices of companies which had leased them, from shipping trucks, and from the factories in which they were manufactured. Xerox Corporation hired scores of private detectives, over the years, to track down this phenomenon of the vanishing Xerox machines, with no significant results. What the officials of the Xerox Corporation did not realize was that if they stopped merely leasing machines and started selling them outright, this problem would be largely solved.

It seemed that nowhere else in the immediate Galaxy were there machines constructed which were capable of doing what Xerox machines did as efficiently as they did it. Hence, any wealthy individual with any interplanetary connections at all and who had some use for the Xerox Corporation's products, did business with a group of pirate Xerox exporters based in the Alpha Centauri star system. These pirates also legally bought and sold huge quantities of Earth photographic, recording, and amplification devices which were also without peer in the immediate Galaxy. They would have been happy simply to buy Xerox copiers as well, but since these machines were not for sale, stealing seemed their only reasonable recourse.

The Master was the proud owner of six Xerox copiers of various models, including a duplicate of the one that stood in the secretarial pool on the eighth floor of the Galaxy Building. At this moment, Superman was acting a great deal like this Xerox machine.

Luthor would unwind his rolls and flash his piles of plastic and paper read-out material past Superman's face. Superman would glance over them much more quickly than any Xerox copier did. A major difference between Superman's behavior and that of a Xerox copier was that once Superman imprinted all of what was apparently nonsense on his mind, he would not immediately forget it.

"Can you make any sense out of it?"

"Shh!" Superman sat on the bed with two fingers pinching the bridge of his nose. It was the first time he had felt safe in Luthor's presence with his eyes closed since they were teenagers. "I think—"

"Everything's there, right? All the stuff I said? Was I right about it?"

"I'm trying to figure out the mathematical code. I think I've got it."

"Are you familiar with the twenty-six brands of Moroccan coffee?"

The Kryptonian didn't question the crack, probably didn't hear it. He talked again after a few moments, "I think I know where the time-snatcher is."

"Where?"

"In a tight orbit around Vega, maybe 40 or 42 million kilometers from the star."

"Do you know exactly where it is now? Can we get there?"

"It's small enough and close enough to the star so that it can't be seen from any observatory in the star system, and it's camouflaged by the overpowering light of Vega. I can find it."

"Want to sabotage it? Do you know how it works?"

"You can figure it out when we get there. It's got a control cab that reproduces the atmosphere of Oric."

"I can stand a little more ammonia for a while."

"If you found out all the Master's secrets, can't he ask the computer banks what information you asked for and figure out what we're up to?

"I told you, as an intelligence gatherer he's strictly bush. You feed this gibberish code into a computer terminal and it automatically forgets the last command it carried out. You just say, "scramble pattern pipeline yellow' and nobody knows you've been snooping unless he was monitoring you at the time."

"You're a good man, Lex Luthor. Ever thought of going into the hero business?"

"Nah, you never get a chance to sleep late. Listen, Supe, I can get out of here easy, but have you given any thought to smuggling yourself to the nearest exit?"

"I've got an idea. This data gave me a pretty good picture of the layout of this pyramid. We're on the first level below the ground level, right?"

"I think so."

"Is there anyone guarding this room? Someone about my size?"

"One guy almost as big as you, but he's got three legs."

"Here's where I show you some super-speed tailoring. Can you mug him and bring me his clothes?"

"Piece of cake. He doesn't look like he's ever worked on a rock pile."

27

This Way Out

Algren Eighteen liked to think that the Cerulean third of his personality was the dominant one. That was where he got his ambitiousness. The other two thirds of Algren Eighteen was Tripedal, which was why when he entered the service of the Master he started as a library guard. Tripedals were dexterous and fiercely responsible, though not noted for their intelligence. Ceruleans, on the other hand, were among the shrewdest races on Oric, and probably the wealthiest. It was only their remarkable lack of any racial loyalty to speak of that allayed any fears among the general population that the seven or eight hundred thousand Ceruleans on Oric might pool their wealth into one of the Galaxy's most powerful economic cartels.

The Ceruleans had six sexes; the Tripedals had three. Consequently the mating exercise that produced Algren Eighteen was composed of two Tripedals and two Ceruleans. The Tripedals undoubtedly thought the entire proceding was a touch kinky. As a result, Algren Eighteen turned out trisexual. Be that as it may.

He was now chief of the attendants at the Master's launching deck two levels below the pyramid's base. He was still only guarding things, but he was rising fast. Apparently his position would become more important as time passed; at any rate the deck was being used a lot more than it used to be when Algren Eighteen was first transferred here.

He supervised six other guards and kept records of the comings and goings of the Master's vehicles with the assistance of his very own assigned portable computer terminal that followed him on wheels while he was on duty and whose red light flashed on to activate it at the sound of Algren Eighteen's voice. He did not give his computer a name.

Algren Eighteen was even more ambitious than all that. There was a windfall coming, and Algren Eighteen knew that the Master was going to be sharp enough to be at the top of it. There were beings of great affairs flocking to Oric these days from the farthest reaches of the Galactic Arm, sometimes even beyond. What about that bare-headed humanoid with the filtrum, Algren Eighteen thought; he must be from clear out at the Central Cluster. He heard the Chief Speaker in the temple go on about the opening of a new age in our lifetimes. The educated beings these days spouted something about an eight-billion-year-old prophesy made by Sonnabend himself. And bigwigs in the organization lurked in corridors muttering to each other about the Future, as if it were some corporeal presence to be awaited like a cosmic dust cloud or the guy who relieves you on the next shift. If they were all planning to be ready to move up, then so would Algren Eighteen. In his spare time he was teaching himself to pilot the Master's vehicles.

The problem was that when he finally figured out how

to bank the surface cruiser into the magnetic lines of force, somebody brought in the shuttle bus. Before he had the time to decipher the controls of the unwieldy machine that transported up to seventy-five medium-sized beings from world to world there were the teleport casters. Teleportation itself was not hard to master, but there was the problem of making sure the object or creature that was teleported did not materialize in solid rock —or in the space of another creature. And then there was the fleet of interstellar jaunters, which were single-passenger craft piloted by remote control from Oric. Algren Eighteen finally caught up with his local technology and got a handle on all this machinery; now he hoped to play with the new device, a black bulb surrounded by eight coiled arms, whose function he could only begin to guess. When night came, he would have a chance to transport this vehicle up the undersea launch ramp and experiment. That was, if traffic down here let up by then.

The day's work was nonstop. Craft were running in and out of the deck like communicable diseases. He was collecting written and oral coded authorization information and feeding it into his computer terminal for each entry and departure. He recorded the time, position of the planet with regard to Vega, course and purpose of each voyage. The data were an unholy mess, sitting inside that animate machine. When he was off duty, before he laid his three hands on that new vehicle, Algren Eighteen would organize it all into a coherent daily log.

"You there, you in charge here?" Algren Eighteen spun in the direction of the voice. It was the new humanoid. The bareheaded one with the filtrum.

"Yes, sir. May I help you?" Algren Eighteen saw that the humanoid was accompanied by another larger one whom he should probably have recognized as one of the Master's attendants. He was in the uniform of a menial and of course had no filtrum. All these humanoids looked alike, it seemed.

"There isn't a moment to spare," the bald one rushed through his words. "We're taking the Black Widow."

"The what?"

"The Black Widow. This one. The vehicle with the bulb. We can both fit. Don't worry, my friend has top clearance." The two humanoids were upon the new vehicle.

"Halt. Hold it there. You need authorization. What is the purpose of your departure?"

"Listen to the pretzel-brain, he wants authorization. Look, mucous-face, while you stand here playing petty bureaucrat, Superman is zooming halfway to Oa to alert the Guardians and the Green Lantern Corps and the Galactic Tribunal and God, for all I know, to the fact that your boss, my boss, the boss of bosses who owns you and everything you see is up to something with a touch of unholiness. Get that weapon out of my face or you'll be scratching for worms with the rest of the turkeys before morning."

"Superman?"

"Right. Very good. Tomorrow we learn to spell cat. Superman's gotten out. And don't tell me you didn't know the Master had him here. The news about how the boss and I captured him is probably halfway to the next Galaxy with that cockamamie clown poet by now."

"Yes, I knew that. But the alert systems—"

"—will very likely be in operation by the time the old flyboy's sprinting into the Central Cluster. I'm the one who tracked him down before. It's only through the incompetence of some idiot like you that he's away now. And if you make me wait for your meshugenah coded authorization the best-laid plans of prophets and kings are going the way of the tyrannosaurus and the dodo, which seems to be making a dramatic comeback right here in this room."

"I do not understand the translation of what you just—"

"You do not understand a whole lot. It was all I could do to enlist this burly specimen in my aid." The outspoken one pointed to the dull-looking humanoid menial at his side. "How many vehicles left here in the past ten minutes?"

"Ten minutes? Computer," the red light went on, "how many vehicles left here in the past—"

"I don't want numbers, you loon. I want to know if you let anyone out of here in that time."

"They're coming and going all the time. At least six beings teleported somewhere, another three were authorized for the various—"

"That kills me. The creep got out right under your nose, or whatever it is you call that banana under your middle eye. Help us get this craft to the hydraulic launch ramp, and I'll think about going easy on you in my report. It's very lightweight. Bulky, but lightweight."

Algren Eighteen gulped, or did something like gulping, and chattered away at his computer terminal as he helped Luthor and the humanoid aide with the Black Widow. "Vehicle designated Black Widow departing coordinates 11:14:50 with reference Vega. Two occupants, both humanoid designated . . ." Algren Eighteen asked the two their names and fed them into the computer terminal ". . . Lex Luthor and Abraham Lincoln."

Bells sounded and lights flashed all over the room. It was the alert system.

"See?" Luthor said. "See? I told you he escaped. Quit feeding that gibberish into the dumbwaiter and set your dials to shoot this cruiser a thousand feet or so over the ocean surface."

Algren Eighteen did that, frantically, as the two humanoids climbed into the open bulb, ready for launch.

"Scramble pattern pipeline yellow," Luthor barked at the computer terminal which immediately began to flash lights and erase information from its banks as the launching ramp hatchway closed and the Black Widow lifted off in the direction of the star Vega.

"What?" Algren Eighteen asked.

"Not a bad escape plan for an amateur," Luthor told his companion as solar energy took over from inertia to fuel the Black Widow.

"Well, it was you who got all that computer information, like the pyramid's layout and the way to scramble the computer record of the escape," Superman complimented Luthor as he tore off the fake uniform and the wad of flattened building material he had scooped out of a wall and used to cover the cleft of his upper lip.

"And you're awfully cute when you smile. Now I suggest you get your bulk out of here so I have the elbow room to pilot this thing before those goons down there figure out where we went."

Superman opened the bulb hatch to do a swan dive upward, and raced the cruiser to the edge of space.

28

The Edge

Luthor had an entire employee whose job it was to read huge quantities of published material and make daily lists of ideas that Luthor had not yet come up with. His name was Arthur Allen, and he was the most successful graduate of the Evelyn Wood School of Reading Dynamics in the year 1971, raising his reading speed from 630 to about 30 thousand words per minute. John Stuart Mill, the nineteenth-century philosopher, read about that fast and came close to going mad because he was incapable of turning pages quickly enough to keep up with himself. Allen read not only every science fiction story published—before publication, if possible—but every popular how-to-publication, every professional journal, and every trade magazine he knew of. A magazine put out by the Sheet Metal Workers' Union had an idea for a kind of reflective sun deck, which Allen wrote down. It gave Luthor the principle for the camouflage device which caused his in-city headquarters to appear, from the air, to be the penthouse of a plant lover with bizarre tastes in art.

An idea in a fictional story by an astronomer named Arthur C. Clarke was not new. The concept of supplying oxygen to a spaceship with plants that breathed carbon dioxide and gave off oxygen was as old as the first fanciful plans for space stations and family-sized space arks. And when unimaginative little Arthur Allen wrote it down in one of his daily reports, Luthor winced at not having thought of it himself.

Here were some ideas Luthor did think of, but which did not work:

1—An elaborate chemical distillation system which would turn Luthor's exhaled carbon dioxide into oxygen and spray the carbon by-product over the black surface of the starcraft's sails. After two major flights, Luthor estimated, the carbon layer would be thick enough to make it quite impossible to roll in the Black Widow's arms.

2—An oxygen pill about the size of a thousand-milligram capsule of vitamin C, which furnished Luthor's bloodstream with as much oxygen as he would need for an hour. It seemed to work on animals, but the first time Luthor tried it the pill made him higher than a weather balloon for hours.

3—An environmental recycling system which would start with the Black Widow's water supply being broken down to component parts of hydrogen and oxygen. Luthor would breathe the oxygen that he extracted from his excess and excreted water, while the carbon dioxide that was the result of his respiration had nothing to do except suffocate the pilot. In any natural ecosystem these substances would combine to form hydrocarbons in organic matter, the building blocks of new life. The only way there would be new life in this craft was if Luthor gave birth.

It all came down to Arthur Clarke's idea of lining all unused surface space inside the bulb of the craft with green vegetation. In jail, about a year ago, Luthor convinced prison officials that it would be a fine idea for him to teach other prisoners a course in horticulture. While preparing for his various lectures on rhododendrons and backyard tomatoes and wild berries, the scientist managed to clone a seed for a new species of moss which would have the heavest respiration rate of any living thing known to man. When he became tired of teaching his course, Luthor sprayed the prison greenhouse with a fertilizer he developed once as a teenager. It caused the plants to sprout overnight like Jack's beanstalk and rupture several walls of the prison so that Luthor could escape quite sloppily. His moss now lined every square inch of the inner black surface of the bubble and spat out oxygen as fast as Luthor sucked it up. His entire water supply consisted of a three-quart canteen slung over the arm of his pilot's seat.

When Superman stopped moving and started downward from twelve hundred kilometers over Oric, Luthor had to continue upward for another 65 kilometers before he could slow down and circle back. The cushioning system that absorbed the inertia in sudden maneuvers was only so strong, and it was how much inertia Luthor's body could stand which was the main limitation on the Black Widow's speed and performance. Luthor could hear Superman "talking" when the hero was actually vibrating the air inside the capsule a certain way with the power conveniently labeled super-ventriloquism. Superman, however, had to read Luthor's lips to understand what he was saying; the air up here was not thick enough to carry sound waves even to Kryptonian ears.

"What're you looking at?" Luthor asked.

He kept looking.

"Hey, Hot Pants, I'm talking to you."

No response.

"Will you turn your lousy head and answer a simple question?" Luthor banged on the wall of his craft.

To no avail.

"For years I've been trying to sneak past him and now I can't get his attention. Is that justice? Maybe there is a God."

Superman turned to face Luthor and projected the words into the bubble: "We've got trouble."

"Hark. I hear a voice."

"The pyramid is past chaos. They're mobilized. If we don't do something fast, they'll spot us before we get where we're going. The sky is being scanned by satellites, which is why I dropped back down into the upper layer of atmosphere."

"What do you suggest we do?"

"Initiate chaos down there."

"From up here?"

"Chaos has always been one of your special talents, Luthor. How would you cause it if you were still inside the pyramid somewhere?"

"Well, I'd start in the launch ramp," Luthor mouthed through his bubble wall. "I'd have to put that out of commission because that would be their first way to follow us."

"How would you do that?"

"Easy. You know that row of teleportation gadgets in there? Teleporting is like going through locks in a canal. Just as you have to equalize the water level in a canal, you have to equalize air pressure to teleport from one place to another, or else you'll have air rushing through the hole you dig in space to teleport at the speed of a cyclone. You can throw the whole launch ramp out of kilter by turning on all those teleport gadgets to a point in deep space. So much air will be rushing out through them into the vacuum that they'll have to seal off the launch ramp like an airlock."

"Brilliant idea."

"What good does it do us up here?"

"What else would you do?" Superman asked as he directed a series of beams of heat vision, melting a series of control bypass switches over a thousand kilometers away.

"Well, next I'd get to their computer linkups. That one would be easy if we were down there. They have no lockout mechanisms, all you have to do is link up to one terminal with the right codes. Like in this case you'd feed the phrase, 'preempt procedure emerald iodine violet,' and then follow it with whatever nonsense phrases you want all the terminals to spout instead of real information. You just feed it into one terminal."

Superman spoke to Luthor with his ventriloquism, as he simultaneously threw his voice elsewhere: "Preempt procedure emerald iodine violet. Mary had a little lamb, its fleece was white as snow, and everywhere that Mary went the lamb was sure to go."

"What are you babbling about? You sure you're recovered from that stuff they had you doped up with?"

"Sure, I'm fine. Just making conversation. What about the Master's operatives in the real estate offices all over the settled part of the planet? They have some sort of linkup for communications, so that they don't give away the same planet to two buyers—or gift receivers, or whatever they call them here."

"Crazy foam."

"Crazy foam."

"You're reading my lips right. The atmosphere here is even better suited to flash fires than it is on Earth. The air itself burns, and an automatic safety system fills all enclosed spaces with some kind of foam to cool down fires. This foam can conduct life-sustaining operations itself—causes respiration of the skin, feeds intravenously if necessary—at the same time as it smothers ignition of the air."

"Sounds like a great regulation. If somebody could patent that process on Earth, he'd pull down a fortune."

"I was planning on it."

Superman located a dozen and a half little offices on Oric, each suited to a different set of environments, each equipped with crazy foam devices in the walls and ceilings—those that had ceilings. A little spark appeared in the air somewhere inside each one.

"Well," Superman grinned and clapped his hands together as he hung on the edge of space, "shall we go on to the time-snatcher now?"

"What? I thought you said—"

"A momentary aberration. You forget with whom you're dealing, old man."

"Son of a gun."

29

Chaos

Earth humanoids kept each other prisoner all the time. They were constantly fighting and revolting and repressing each other effectively and enthusiastically. They were used to dealing with such things. The Master might very well learn from them. They were more practiced at it than he was, which was why, he supposed, the alarm sounded to signal Superman's escape. The Kryptonian was raised among the wolves and so took on their talents.

Superman would be conscious now, and sentient. It was fortunate that the Master was in his study at the tip of the pyramid. The escaped hero would not be able to see him from wherever he was through the lead sheeting that expensively but unostentatiously lined an inner layer of the study walls.

The Master ordered the reconnaissance satellites operational. All of them. The Tripedal guards began an exhaustive search of every corner and object in the pyramid large enough to hold a humanoid. It was probably Tripedals who were responsible for the escape, the dull-witted creatures. The individuals responsible would be singled out when the emergency was over and requested to offer the Master a gift of satisfaction, doubtless some standard form of self-torture.

The Master tuned one of his study monitors to the launch deck. His enforcement detail was already there.

Six Ceruleans presented the hybrid Algren Eighteen with their emergency traveling orders. They would each occupy one interstellar jaunter and have separate destinations. Their mission would be to find Superman, at any of the six Galactic locations where he might cause the Master the most trouble.

"Will this be in addition to the chase undertaken by . . ." Algren Eighteen jumbled through his mind for the names, for the record in his computer terminal had been mysteriously misplaced, "Lex Luthor and Abraham Lincoln?"

"Who?" the chief of the Cerulean unit asked.

"The hairless humanoid and his aide who took the new vehicle as the alarm was sounding."

"We have no time for explanations," the Cerulean barked—

—as the row of teleporters along the wall activated themselves one by one and drew up everything in the huge hangar like powerful suction cleaners sweeping across a sandy shore.

The Master saw it all. He ordered every Gorgan in the pyramid to teleport immediately to the launch deck. These were very massive beings who would be able to function in that environment of high deadly winds. They were to salvage all valuable equipment not already destroyed and pull the six Ceruleans and seven guards on the launch deck out of there so the room could be sealed off until the teleporters were brought under control. That would take time. It would also take personnel, which seemed suddenly to be at a premium.

The Master got an order, via computer linkup, out to each of the offices of his real estate operations on Oric. "This is to alert you that our Major Plan is to go into effect immediately, ahead of schedule. Chief Operational Officers at each facility are to consult their computer terminals for hitherto secret information about their respective functions in the coming extraordinary period. Code to obtain your orders is as follows: 'Landfill heliotrope.' You may obtain such information now."

The Master ended this message as his own terminal flashed its red light on and off several times for no apparent reason. He thought nothing of it, had no time to think anything of it, had more on his mind.

In eighteen office facilities on Oric the same thing happened to eighteen computer terminals. Eighteen Chief Operational Officers said, in eighteen different languages, "Landfill heliotrope," to their respective terminals. Eighteen terminals answered:

"Mary had a little lamb, its fleece was white as snow, and everywhere that Mary went the lamb was sure to go."

Before any of the officers had the chance to wonder if this was some sort of code, every real estate office belonging to the Master filled up with life-supporting, business-stopping foam.

The Master did not know what had happened in his real estate offices. It would not much matter, actually. Not now. These underlings would do no more than administer his operations on Oric while the Master was fulfilling his destiny across the sky.

A tremor rocked the planet. And another. A tidal wave lapped over the side of the pyramid and nearly reached its peak. The Master looked upward, out the open tip of his study, and saw a pair of what looked to be moons. Oric had no moons. The Master knew what they were, and now he knew where Superman was. The Kryptonian was doing something worse than wasting his own time, he was fate's tool, prodding the Master on to where the prophet Sonnabend said he must go these eons past. It was time to leave.

He had laid in his course long ago. Today was the beginning. A new age was born here and now. The few most trusted and obedient of his attendants were here; they were on their way.

A set of four triangular walls poked up from the open tip of the pyramid and met in a point, sealing the structure closed. The upper forty feet of the pyramid rose as if with a great piano hinge on one side until the tip pointed into the sky at a 60-degree angle with the ground. Then with a great soundless lurch it lifted off the surface of the rest of the structure and soared at the heavens.

The pyramid-shaped spacecraft gained speed and finally ignited as it passed out of Oric's atmosphere. There, ahead somewhere, hidden by the fiery mass of blue Vega, was the device that was causing a spate of worlds to materialize around Oric. Dead husks, duplicates of Oric itself. Oric could die today for all the Master cared, and it well might.

A hundred kilometers from Oric the pyramidal spacecraft shimmered and swirled in a rainbow of smoky colors and seemed to vanish. It made the rest of the trip disguised in an illusion of an infrared wave.

30

Retrieval

"That button over there." The blue-sleeved hand darted to press one of the myriad dials, levers, heat-sensitive bulbs, and other controls lining the six walls of the cramped cab.

"Excuse me, bunkie. Don't you have anything useful to do? We're just a few light-seconds from Vega, why don't you take a steam bath?" Apparently Superman's helpful suggestions as to how the machinery worked were as welcome to Luthor as someone reading over John Stuart Mill's shoulder. It did not take Luthor long at all, for a mortal, to determine how the time-snatcher worked. Superman calculated that they could snatch a maximum of 21 facsimiles without permanently damaging the planet.

Luthor set about reaching a billion years into the future for a collection of Xerox-style copies of the dead husk of the planet Oric which he placed skillfully in orbit around the original like moons. As this process began,

Superman slipped out of the airlock of the contraption and swam through space back to the planet. The idea was to create chaos, but avoid disaster.

Luthor was quite jealous of whoever it was that had designed this time-snatcher. The machine used no basic principles that were unfamiliar to Luthor. The thing simply used what Luthor knew so damned efficiently. There was no margin for error to account for imprecise borders between different dimensions. No energy-matter discrepancy. The time-snatcher dealt with only inorganic matter and could move virtually any amount of it across unlimited expanses of time or space, ignoring the physical laws of the three-dimensional Universe. The navigational equipment of the Black Widow compared to it as a kayak compares to an aircraft carrier.

The Master must certainly have stumbled on this piece of equipment, or stolen it and lost its inventor and anyone who completely understood its mechanism. There was nothing on Oric among the technology provided by a thousand advanced cultures to compare with it. If he could tinker with stuff like this all the time, Luthor thought, he might be content to leave off the nonsense of his life and live out however many years he had as a traveling interplanetary fixit man, if there was such a profession.

The time-snatcher worked so quickly that by the time Superman arrived back at Oric there already were three facsimiles of the planet in orbit around it and a fourth taking shape like a film image coming into focus. The Kryptonian stole a glance at the Master's headquarters and saw nothing unexpected, although he could not see through the walls of the pyramid's upper chambers. Everyone seemed to be occupied with the crises Superman and Luthor had left behind. The teleporters were still turned on, and the computer terminals were still spouting the nursery rhyme, and the various races among the

Master's employees were coping in their respective fashions. The first tidal wave was coming.

There were nine facsimiles drawn back from a billion years in Oric's future, and the tides of ammonia water were heaving toward Cyber Island. There was a heavily populated community mostly made up of Lalofins and Gorgans on the undersea shelf directly in the tidal wave's path. Superman plowed into the putrid ocean like a dagger and swept back and forth along the border between the settlement and the open sea, setting up a cross-current to meet the tidal wave that was half a kilometer away and building.

Superman spanned his 200-meter course twelve times a second, following a pattern through the liquid he mentally calculated as he was diving into it. But when the wave was 300 meters away, Superman sensed that he had not stirred up the ocean enough. It was not churning as it should be, and the undersea community was imminently threatened.

He swept into the sky over the ammonia sea and saw the wave coming, with no cross-current building to neutralize it. The only thing Superman seemed to leave behind was his own wake, foaming at the surface. There were seconds before the tidal wave would surely sweep over the settlement, onto the island itself.

Superman knifed back into the sea and flashed directly at the coming tidal wave. Before he reached it he felt himself swept around by the sea itself like a corkscrew and slammed at the ocean floor. He looked up in time to see the tidal pattern lumbering over his head and pacified by a collection of sonic generators that circled the ocean floor around Cyber for the purpose of doing just that. It was the sonic generators, no doubt, that had caught Superman in their vibrations and unexpectedly mashed him into the muck, that had calmed his cross-current, and that would be routinely catching tidal waves before they reached any populated area of the planet.

Quakes. There would be quakes. There were sixteen Orics in the sky and there were hellish rumblings from thousands of kilometers around the planet.

Superman found one quake with his x-ray vision. He caught sight of the underground plates it was loosening. He traced the probable pattern of quakes to follow. He was ready for them to reach the planet's population, and so was the population ready.

Before the first sign of tremors on Cyber, alarms clanged and lights flashed. Creatures looked up with resigned expressions—those who could form expressions— and scores of entire buildings raised themselves up on great collections of springs. The buildings on springs were equipped with expensive magnetic devices that homed in on the planet's immoveable center of gravity, and when the tremors started the buildings essentially stood still, relative to the planet, while the surface shivered.

The buildings not equipped with springs shot full of life-saving foam. There were nineteen Orics in the sky, and Superman felt quite useless here. The crisis he and Luthor had brought about was certainly most inconvenient for the population of Oric, but hardly dangerous.

The only thing left for Superman to do was to flash through the pyramid and find MacDuff, Luthor's computer terminal, and see what the machine knew about flushing out the Master. This Superman did, swimming undersea through the closed hatch of the launch ramp and into the winds caused by the runaway teleport machines. Superman slammed into each of the machines, disabling and, nominally, turning them off.

MacDuff was inert in the corridor where Luthor's office had been. It would be quicker to fly the terminal to

Luthor himself several million miles away than for Superman to figure out the codes that would reactivate it and then imitate Luthor's voice to do so.

All at super-speed to blur any sight of him Superman wrapped the computer in his protective cape and flew it up above the pyramid . . .

. . . and the pyramid had no point. The Master was gone, along with all his intentions.

Superman and the computer-terminal crashed a space warp directly at the star Vega. The hero was inside the time-snatcher again in less than 30 seconds of real time.

"The Master's gone," he told Luthor before the scientist knew he was back, "took off somewhere. Can you trace him?"

What followed were seconds wasted annoyingly, several useless words in abbreviated conversation, startled instants, and random feed-outs from the computer. There were checks and double-checks that always came out the same and were thus even more annoying in their original accuracy.

The battle on Oric was over, and Superman and Luthor had apparently won it, if only by default. The answer from the computer was the same each time. The course was locked in long ago. The Master had gone to Earth.

31

The Coincidence

The scene struck Luthor as extremely funny. He
He laughed so hard he had to hold his stomach in with
both hands.

There stood the biggest genuine legend Luthor had
ever met, surrounded in this time-snatcher cab by the
super-scientific technology of the Galactic Arm. This
Man of Steel had bested all that surrounded him. He had,
at least for the moment, confounded a brilliantly con-
ceived and nearly executed scheme for massive conquest.
A scheme that still might prove successful, owing in
large part to this lunk-headed hero's amazing lack of
imagination.

"Well, I don't see what's so funny, Luthor. I just said
I think it's a trap. It's too much of a coincidence for
Earth to be the Master's planned starting point for his
takeover."

Luthor fell off his chair, trying to catch his breath,
laughing.

"Keep up that heavy respiration, Luthor, and you'll use up your oxygen supply."

He laughed some more.

"I mean, if you were the Master and you wanted to get somebody like me out of the way, wouldn't you go somewhere where I'd feel on home territory to spring your trap?"

"You hopeless loon! I thought I was conceited, but—" Luthor lost his breath again and rolled over, nearly belching out his diaphragm.

"The Universe is sinking slowly down around our ankles, and you think it's a laugh."

"Listen—" he broke up again.

After a few moments Luthor snatched back his composure long enough to tell his strange ally what he thought was going on.

"You think you're the only thing that's happening on Earth, don't you?" Luthor's tone became accusatory.

"What do you mean?"

"I mean you're always accusing me of trying to make myself emperor of Earth, aren't you?"

"You've practically admitted it."

"I've said there are less worthy pursuits for someone of my intelligence and talent."

"If you say so."

"There are worlds around with greater natural resources, more developed wealth. You know that. And worlds without super-heroes parading around the place in funny clothes making sure nobody's tougher than they are. And I think I've made it clear that I'm altogether capable of finding and conquering myself a planet or two."

"I'll concede that point."

"But I've hung around Earth for a reason. I don't know why you kick around the place looking for work yourself if you haven't realized that what's happening on

Earth right now is something any conqueror would give his Captain Video secret code ring to have."

"I'm afraid I don't think along those lines. What are you talking about?"

"I'm talking about a global culture whose scientific wealth has outstripped by a light-year its social and political development in just one or two generations. I'm talking about a race with a population of humans that the planet manages to support far beyond its apparent ability to do so. I'm talking about four billion—count 'em—four billion intelligent, incredibly industrious creatures. Capable of making decisions, with the manual dexterity to tie knots and pull triggers, who can navigate courses and plan complicated procedures over periods of not only the next hour or the next day, but the next century. What's the intelligent population of the planet Regulus-6?"

"About 760 million."

"And at what stage of scientific development are they?"

"Last time I was there, someone had just figured out the steam turbine."

"And it'll be centuries before anyone comes up with the idea of putting it to use in transportation or trade."

"When were you on Regulus-6?"

"Remember when I broke out of jail last year and nobody knew where I was for three weeks?"

"You went to Regulus-6?"

"Give the man a cigar."

"I'm impressed."

"Listen. The population boom on Earth has gotten out of hand. There are whole cities—countries—continents—full of people aching for something useful to do with their lives. Talented, intelligent people. And what's more, the whole cockamamie world is wired for sight and sound. There isn't a grain of sand on the globe that doesn't have radio waves slicing through it, cauterizing it with electronic mumbo-jumbo twenty-four hours a day. The first Hitler type that can coordinate all that communications paraphernalia has the immediate Galaxy's greatest living resource in the palm of his hand. And if it's title to the Galactic Arm the guy wants, then all he's got to do is convince all these intelligent, obedient, bored creatures that it'd be a kick to go off and do some heavy conquering for him. It worked with the Crusades, and look at all the trouble that caused."

"If you've realized that all along, why haven't you done it yourself?"

Luthor was beyond amusement. "What the sizzling suns do you think you've been keeping me from doing all these years, Jocko, playing Monopoly?"

"Great Krypton!"

"You talk funnier than I do, you self-righteous lunk. That hybrid clown isn't on Earth to trap you. He's there despite you. And the longer you stay here worrying about it, the likelier it's going to be that he'll be able to—"

But Superman was gone, and Luthor wondered why the big guy kept winning.

Luthor had work to do, too. If those twenty-one facsimiles of the planet Oric were allowed to continue hanging there in orbit much longer, the original would inevitably turn into space dust in a cataclysm visible clear to Andromeda. As long as he was going about setting straight the balance of worlds today instead of dismembering them, Luthor supposed, he might just as well put everything here back the way it belonged before he went home. Besides that, there was something on Oric he had to pick up before he left.

The big Videobeam television screen in the sidewalk window next to the main entrance of the Galaxy Building was the first thing that struck Clark Kent as odd. Dan Reed, the newscaster who generally substituted for Clark during vacations, was on the air with the 4:55 P.M.

billboard. This was the five-minute summary of news headlines to be expanded upon an hour later on the evening news.

As Reed signed off he said, "This is Dan Reed with Wednesday's headlines from the WGBS newsroom. Join me for the full report one hour from now."

Wednesday. Was it possible that Superman had miscalculated his space-warp travel and returned to Earth a day before he left Oric, or was the station simply running a tape of yesterday's news for some reason?

Clark stepped into the lobby for a newspaper. Yes, it was Thursday, all right.

32

The Takeover

"Back from your vacation early, aintcha, Mr. Kent?" the lobby newsdealer said.

"Just a few days. Though I'd take the rest of this week off later in the year, Jack."

"Well, you're back none too soon. Your friends been actin' awful weird all day."

"How so?"

"Well, like that Lombard guy. Y'know, the one with all the girlfriends?"

"I know which one you mean."

"He come in this morning, bought a paper, said 'good morning,' and went on up the elevator."

"What's weird about that?"

"Well, every morning since he got his job here he's walked in, said 'Hi, Jack, how's tricks?' and tried to pass me a nickel for a quarter paper. Then he laughs like it's a big joke and goes off. Every morning like clockwork."

"Hi, Jack, how's tricks?"

"At first I said something like, 'She's fine, how's Agnes?' but he didn't notice. He'd just laugh and go off."

"He would."

"Yep. 'Hi, Jack, how's tricks?' Rest of the TV people were a little screwy, too. Like that nice Miss Lane who's all go-get-em all the time? She walked in prim and proper as can be, says 'good morning' just like Lombard, and walks to the elevator like nothing's wrong."

"So?"

"So? Miss Lane don't come in till four in the afternoon, that's so. She always knew what time it was before. Everybody said 'good morning,' and that's all. No matter what time of day it was."

"Thanks, Jack," Clark said, walking to the elevators. "I'm sure it's nothing, just nerves."

"Nerves. I dunno, Mr. Kent, I always said of all those screwy TV guys you were the only normal one."

The twentieth floor was naked as a ghost town. Even the wire service machines were silent. Clark walked into the hall, past the receptionist.

"Good morning," the girl said.

Clark strode down the hall to his office, passing open doors with a person at a desk behind each one. Hands clasped, eyes front, faces pleasantly blank. Clark was the most animated, interesting person in the entire television operation. He greeted the faces behind the open office doors as he passed them. "Good morning," each one said.

The Master was surely on Earth somewhere. Or near it. Every television and radio station would be like this by now, every telegraph and telephone office, its personnel somehow mesmerized. Waiting. Clark ambled into Steve Lombard's office, sat down, and put his feet up on the desk.

"Good morning, Clark," Lombard said pleasantly.

"Hi, you dumb jock," Clark answered. "How's tricks?"

"Fine, thank you, and yourself?"

"Nothing new. Had a pretty good vacation, just flew in from Vega. Fought off an army of rocket-powered robots and saved a planet from blowing up this morning before breakfast."

"That's nice."

"Tell me, Steve, you overblown fool, what's everybody waiting around for?"

"The address."

"Whose address?"

"The Master's."

"When's that?"

"Six P.M. eastern time."

"Am I correct in assuming that he has managed to tie in all media on the planet to some broadcast facility of his own?"

"I don't know."

"Has he allowed for simultaneous translation over the airwaves using those language devices everyone on his home planet wears?"

"I don't know."

"Don't know much, do you, Grizzly? Tell me, when he got you all under his power, did you get to see what he

217

looked like, this mysterious Master? Did he show you his face on a monitor screen of some sort?"

"He has four arms and a large mustache," Lombard said in a monotone. " 'Gainst his rule need for freedom sure will fade."

"I thought so." Clark leaned back. "By the way, Stevie-boy, while I've got you here, and since we have nearly an hour before the broadcast, there are some things I've been meaning to tell you."

"Yes, Clark?"

"For example, did you know you were a conceited jerk with delusions of self-worth?"

"Yes, Clark."

"And that you are quite incapable of feeling much of anything for anyone but yourself, and so you compensate by being aggressive and obnoxious?"

"Yes, Clark."

"And that bet we've got going, about the relative appeal of your Bloody Mary and my mother's special soft drink formula, remember that?"

"Yes, Clark."

"Well, the fix is in. It's rigged, you see, and you're going to be awfully embarrassed when you can't have enough of my soft drink."

"Yes, Clark."

"Let's see now. What did I leave out . . . ?"

In a synchronized orbit 22 thousand miles over the Atlantic Ocean the Master and his slaves made a final check of the content of the Master's broadcast. It would do the job, the Master concluded.

At precisely 6 P.M. Eastern Time the Master was poised in his warp vehicle before a sophisticated broadcast camera. He began to speak.

In San Francisco a young woman named Linda Fentiman was watching television. The picture rolled momentarily as an unfamiliar face came on the screen and said,

"This is Clark Kent with the WGBS News from Metropolis . . ."

In the Chinese province of Kwangtung a boy named Hua Lo-Feng rode a bicycle and listened to a small radio strapped to the handlebar as he heard an unfamiliar voice speak in fluent Cantonese, ". . . today's lead story concerns the apparent takeover by an alien financier of all mass communications facilities on Earth . . ."

Over the airport in Johannesburg, South Africa, Charles Belleville, a French pilot, and Kwame Niiga, a fight controller, were interrupted on their shortwave communication by a voice they heard speaking respectively French and Afrikaans, ". . . the alien is a native of the Vega star system and is reputedly known to Superman, who made this broadcast possible . . ."

And in telephone conversations all over the world, in languages and dialects uncounted, conversations were interrupted by ". . . details later in the show. . . ."

A thunderous crack of sound interrupted Clark Kent's broadcast, and several feet in front of the reporter, among three dazed technical workers who were the only people in Studio B with Clark, lights and smoke of all colors began to swirl.

The colors collected and hardened into the form of Towbee, the minstrel from space, his once elfin face twisted with determination and rage.

"I am the Master," Towbee said, "and I assume you are prepared to die." He had no disguise to drop but his madness.

33

In My Father's Eyes

Before anything else happened, Clark heat-beamed all communications lines out of the studio and he sucked most of the oxygen from the room so that the three dazed technicians fell unconscious.

"Let us reason this out," Towbee said as he raised the hands of two arms. "I am the product of scores of races and nearly a thousand cultures, I am one of the most sophisticated and powerful individuals in the Galaxy, I have powers and abilities beyond your imagination. You, on the other hand, are reputedly the most formidable and resourceful single being known to inhabit the Milky Way in thousands of years; in legendary exploits recounted in dialects of every star that has spawned intelligence you have not suffered a significant defeat since the destruction of your home world; your coming was foretold by the prophet Sonnabend himself.

"If you say so," Clark responded.

"On the basis of that alone, there is probably an even chance for either of us to defeat the other."

"A gambler friend of mine says fifty-fifty is good odds."

"But," the alien pointed one of his four index fingers, "that selfsame prophet also predicted my own coming, a hybrid born to Vega with an empire based on trade, you will remember. There is no doubt that I am the being of whom Sonnabend spoke. The time to which he referred has come, and I am the only hybrid on Vega whose intelligence and authority are even close to that of a potential ruler. This prophet whose words have for billions of years proved flawless has said I will defeat all opposition, even your own. When you take that added factor into account, good Superman, would it not seem prudent to forget your bravado and join my service?"

"Your reasoning is as flawless as Sonnabend's prophesies, Towbee." Clark Kent walked out from behind his anchor desk. "But we shall see just how flawless that actually is."

The reporter flexed every boulder-shaped muscle on the surface of his body and the anchorman's conservative blue suit ripped and unraveled in a hundred places until there were just loose threads falling all over the floor around the breathtaking figure of Superman.

Towbee was braced for the attack as the Man of Steel dived unexpectedly past the minstrel at the two cameramen and the sound technician who lay on the floor behind him. Superman snapped up the technician and one cameraman and whisked them away from the brewing battle, into the partitioned audience section that is used only when Studio B is transformed from newsroom to variety show set.

Towbee had no idea that the hero's vaunted respect for life extended so far as to hinder his own performance in the face of an enemy. The alien used the free millisecond to his advantage, dancing a finger over certain keys of his instrument to shoot a bolt of light at the skull of the remaining cameraman who lay dazed on the news set.

As Superman dropped the two unconscious men into padded audience chairs and began to turn around, he had to decide (1) what he had to do to defeat Towbee and (2) how Towbee proposed to defeat him. The second question was clear by the time Superman was fully turned to face the studio proper where the villain stood.

His momentum through the air was already building when in his path, between himself and the malevolent clown, a hold opened in the very fabric of space and there was no way Superman could avoid careening into it with the speed of a Jovian tornado. He would be lost somewhere in the infinite folds of time and space and for all his powers—if wherever he found himself he would have any powers—he could never find his way back home. In mid-flight he whipped the cape from his back.

He whirled the red stretchable cloth over his head as he flew across the scant feet separating him from oblivion. The indestructible fabric twisted and spun like a flag in a cyclone, but it held. It stretched the length and breadth of the huge room, slicing through wall consoles and two television cameras, over the hole in space around the throat of the trap-setter on the other side, and as Superman fell headlong at the void the startled Towbee yanked on the cape with a neck and four arms mighty beyond their appearance, pulling the last son of Krypton back to the plane of Earth and flinging him through a battery of monitors and the wall of the studio as well.

Superman lay on his back in the director's control room, still clutching his cape in his right fist, his eyes closed with unconsciousness for the merest fraction of an instant. He opened them to see a dozen red thunderbolts streaking out of Towbee's image machine, directly at his head. Superman sprang upward and flew, his back scraping the ceiling, over, under, around the flashes near lightspeed. The villain was his now. He would get close enough to overpower him with sheer might like a veteran boxer momentarily snowed by a quick opponent's flashy tricks, but who managed to weather them all. Two fists clenched together, the indestructible cape still trailing behind them like a truck's danger signal. There was no gimmick the alien could juggle from his instrument in time. As he tumbled at the enemy Superman glanced at the dimensional rip still dangling in the air; the remaining dazed cameraman was halfway into it.

Superman altered his direction, missing Towbee, snatching the cameraman's leg in the crook of his cape, hoping whatever bizarre laws prevailed on the other side of the divide would allow the man's return alive. They did. The hero whisked the man toward his colleagues in the rows of seats, flying slowly enough so that the man's skin would not burn with friction, slowly enough to give him a chance to claw up the cape and slam an elbow into Superman's steely face, crushing the elbow hopelessly.

Towbee had obviously done something to the man's mind while Superman wasn't looking. He was fighting like a trapped animal, cracking his knuckles on Superman's chest, mashing toes into his legs, and Superman could not stop him from hurting himself while he got the man to his seat. The man was not thinking; no one in the entire television operation had been capable of thought since Towbee's takeover of the broadcast media. The mortal must be driven by nervous energy and Towbee's impulses to him.

With the skill of an acupuncturist Superman ran a diamond-hard fingernail down the cameraman's spinal cord. The man fell limp, his central nervous system temporarily paralyzed. When Superman turned back to Towbee's direction, the door through space was gone, but Superman faced his father Jor-El.

The images of Towbee's instrument took on the character of the original, along with whatever other traits the musician cared to add. The figure of hardened smoke and light standing beside the only television camera still intact was Jor-El, over seven feet tall, and his eyes brimming with disdain.

"No son of mine flies all over the Universe looking for trouble to meddle in," and Jor-El flung up a powerful Kryptonian arm to swat his son through the divider to the audience where he landed, squashing four seats as he ruptured the floor.

Around him Superman heard titters, then chuckles, then laughter, then guffaws, then he opened his eyes and he was surrounded, in the audience, by three hundred Towbees, sitting and laughing as if at a Marx Brothers routine, but laughing at him. Superman. Little Kal-El.

"Let that be a lesson to you," Jor-El said, standing bigger than life in front of the audience section, ignoring the raucous laughter of the Towbee forms. Which one was real?

"What do you want?" the dazed, disoriented Superman squeaked as he got up, bottom first in the manner of a small boy.

"I want you to apologize, and then go to your room," Jor-El boomed as hundreds of Towbees cackled, clouding Superman's mind. "I want you to go right to your room."

Jor-El pointed in the direction of a small swirling point in front of Superman's face. A point that stretched and enlarged and became another doorway to somewhere in time and space. Kal-El's room?

"I'm sorry, Daddy."

The form and the voice were those of Jor-El. Superman even heard the words in the Kryptonese language that only he remembered, but could these really be the words of Jor-El?

Superman was standing, listing to either side like an embarrassed child wishing he would fall into the floor. Jor-El must be really angry to talk like that, but angry at what? Was it Jor-El who should be angry?

"Why did you send me away!" the man-child in red and blue suddenly screamed.

"To your room."

"You sent me away. You never came and got me again. I was hungry that whole time. I didn't want to go. You sent me away and there was noise and it got dark and I couldn't get to sleep because I was scared and I cried. Why did you send me away?"

"You ungrateful little brat."

Three hundred Towbees laughed.

"I had my reasons," Jor-El boomed, "and they are not for you to question. To your room." He pointed at the growing hole to oblivion.

It was an order. He must obey it. Why?

He was little Kal-El, and he must listen to his father.

He was timid Clark Kent, and he must pay attention to all authority figures.

He was a failed hero, about to be overcome by someone stronger.

No.

He was Superman, by God. Towbee, Superman realized, Towbee wasn't one of these round huffing little figures in the audience. Towbee was there—in front of him —urging him to his doom—dressed in the form of his father.

There was an evil in this place and for all he had ever been or hoped to be, Superman was going to defeat that evil.

That was the last coherent thought he had.

Later, gradually, Superman remembered seeing himself spring up at the false form of his father like a bolt of nova light. Never in his life had Superman felt his physical self so dominate his being. There was a moment in a swirl of colors, smoke and light kicking around the room in a manic nonsensical pattern. The whole thing was over in a time too short to measure.

The next thing he clearly saw was his father's face, with Superman's own hands clenched around the throat, fading into that of the space minstrel. And he heard a voice.

"You have done well, Kal-El. Your job is through."

He ignored the voice. It was all he was capable of doing at this moment, as his mind floated back to the control of his muscles.

"Loosen your grip, Kal-El. You may hurt him permanently, and you do not do that. We can deal with him now."

He loosened his grip, and the hybrid being lay on the floor of what remained in the studio. Superman looked in the direction of the soft hand that held his shoulder. It was the Old-Timer. He knew it was really the Old-Timer. There was no doubt.

"You have done well, my son."

"I'm not your son."

"My friend. You have broken the eight-billion-year run of Sonnabend's prophesies. If not for you, dire predictions of Galactic calamity beginning at this time and place would surely have come true. But you have stemmed the disastrous flow of history, and we stand on the threshold of an age undreamed of by any prophet. There certainly will be a long struggle ahead, but the forces of good now have a chance to prevail. The Galaxy thanks you, Kal-El, and welcomes you to the ranks of its greatest heroes."

Superman was beginning to understand. Not quite, but he was beginning. He remembered a piece of an old line and said to the former Guardian, "If there is a place and work for me, then I am ready." He thought a moment, "Lincoln said that, didn't he?"

"Yes," Old-Timer said, "Lincoln."

Superman looked up at the wall of the studio and realized he would have to repair it and see to that cameraman's broken bones. A wall clock that was still running told him that since Towbee entered the studio a minute and twenty seconds had passed.

On the roof of the Galaxy Building the Black Widow landed. Lex Luthor stepped out in his full outlandish costume and walked to the stairway door that Old-Timer had left open for him.

34

Restoration

His voice was rich and authoritative; his face inspired trust, a symbol of honor and justice even to those who had made themselves his adversaries. Superman was certainly the most suitable host possible for this particular worldwide multilingual broadcast.

"When I snap my fingers it is your signal that I have finished my message. You will then slip from this hypnotic state into normal sleep. You will nap until you feel rested and you will remember only that part of these experiences about which you feel comfortable. When you wake up you will do so freely and easily and you will feel fine about everything that has happened today, you will have no lingering effects from these events. I will count down from three and snap my fingers. Three, two, one . . ."

"I appreciate the help, Lex. Really," the Kryptonian said as Luthor shut down the color television camera. The lately pardoned felon served as engineer and technical adviser, combining his knowledge of broadcast hardware with Superman's computer-like mind to reconstruct Towbee's massive communications network in less than an hour so that the hero could address the dazed media employees around the Earth. The two would make their peace with the unions later.

"Say no more, Noodles. See you around."

"You going somewhere?"

"No, actually I thought I'd wait around here for the world to wake up so some rookie cop could give me a ticket for double-parking my star cruiser."

"You've got a full Presidential pardon now. What are you going to do with it?"

"I'm planning on settling down, getting a house in the suburbs, joining the Rotary and the PTA. How should I know what I'm going to do?"

"There must be something on your mind."

"Right now I'm going to get that contraption off the roof and back to the Modern Art Museum where it belongs when it's not flying through space. What should I be doing?"

"Well, there is the Einstein document that's still not

accounted for. I suppose I'll have to go back to Oric and look for it."

"Listen, standing around shooting the breeze with you is my second favorite pastime, but those technicians all over the studio floor are starting to come out of their trances and your reporter friend Kent is liable to turn up here any minute and I don't feel like granting any interviews just now. I'll take the elevator to the roof."

"I'll drop you." Superman swept the scientist off his feet and before he could catch a cold Luthor found himself standing in front of his arachnoid spacecraft. "What's first?" Superman asked.

"First?"

"You told me your second favorite pastime. What's first?"

"Having an unclean yak sit on my dinner."

"Johnny Carson, 1967."

"Right. I forgot about your total recall. Well, see you around, physical one."

"Can I give the Black Widow a boost?"

"No, I'll just roll it off the rooftop. It's got enough energy stored up to get back to the museum courtyard on its own. Bye."

"Sure you're not up to getting that document back from Oric? Philistine hands, you called them, didn't you?"

"I've had enough of that alien nonsense for a while. There's probably nothing much the old fiddler could've said I don't already know, anyhow. That stuff the Master thought about Einstein's finding a way to trisect an angle is a lot of hokum. I'll be going now."

"Have a good trip," Superman said and stood there as if expecting something.

Luthor thought of asking him if he's leaving or posing for the pigeons, but he didn't pursue it. Luthor opened the dome of the Black Widow's bubble, climbed in, and

229

as he began closing the dome Superman hopped off the side of the building and vanished from sight.

The Black Widow needed only a few seconds to warm up. Luthor raised the sails and soaked solar energy before he pulled them back in, rolled the arms tightly against the bubble and shifted his own weight inside so that the mechanism rolled over and tumbled toward the edge of the roof and off. Less than halfway down the side of the 70-story building, while the sails were still unfurling, the vehicle stopped itself, started upward and instead of continuing to rise, froze motionless 350 feet over Governor's Plaza.

Luthor pressed buttons. Turned dials. Took readings. He threw open the dome of the bubble and leaped out, jet boots hissing his anger, as he flew at the huge red-and-blue-costumed figure holding the craft over his head like Atlas supporting the world.

"What the flying moonballs do you think you're doing?" Luthor said it in under half a second.

"Taking you in. Sorry old man."

"This is private property, Creepo. Get your filthy alien mitts off it. I'm a citizen now. I've got rights."

"Don't huff at me, Luthor. The document is stashed in its lead case in the pillow under your pilot seat. The same pillow I was lying on in my interrogation cell on Oric. I've known that since you landed. I also figured out on the way back to Earth that what the Master wanted from me was the knowledge of the written Kryptonese language, the language in which Einstein wrote that letter. I figured that out from the dreams I had when I was under interrogation. I also figured out that you knew that from the inquiries you made of your robot computer. I've been giving you the benefit of the doubt all this time, hoping you'd break down and give it back."

"So you've got me on a charge the pardon didn't cover. You have more smarts than I gave you credit for."

"I always did. That's where you've generally gone wrong."

"Well, I'm not going to go wrong this time—" Luthor poised a fisted right glove in Superman's direction, about to press the button on the second knuckle to unleash whatever fearsome weapon it controlled.

"Hold it, Luthor. Let's reason this out."

"Talk fast, hero."

"We're hovering here a few hundred feet over the city," Superman said no faster than he felt like talking. "You've got more crazy gadgets lining your outfit than a stage magician, and I don't know what most of them are. On top of that, I'm holding this flier of yours with both hands and I'll be careful of it because it will be necessary as evidence. On the other hand, I've still got my super powers and they've always been able to defeat you one-on-one before. On the basis of that alone, I'll be liberal and give you an even chance of winning out over me. Agreed?"

"So far."

"Now, add to that the fact that I'm pretty much still flushed with a victory over a would-be despot whose coming was apparently foretold eight billion years ago. I just knocked off the prediction of a guy who's had a perfect win-loss record since the beginning of recorded time. Unless you suppose I'm going to let a mere mortal with a funny costume that isn't even as good as mine ruin my day, I suggest you forget the bravado and give yourself up."

In the final analysis Lex Luthor was, after all, a creature of reason, not heroics. Superman had some hope that the brilliant scientist would wait at the Pocantico State Correctional Facility until his trial for the relatively minor crime of concealing the document. With the hero's testimony a case could probably be made that this was a crime of passion, the theft of an artifact from the life of an idol and not a cold-blooded criminal act.

But Luthor would not stand still waiting for any court

proceedings. Within the familiar confines of prison, the familiar behavior patterns would find their way home.

35

The Gift

The inoffensively handsome face would speak to a worldwide television audience for the second time in the past day. In a conference room in the Galaxy Building Clark Kent looked remarkably ill at ease as his colleagues from newspapers and broadcast news departments on three continents questioned him about the extraordinary broadcast of yesterday evening. Superman was unavailable, of course; Luthor was the last one to see him and the criminal had requested that he be placed in solitary confinement until the whole affair blew over. So Clark was famous today.

"I simply happened to be caught at the culmination of a series of events," Clark shrugged. "It's in my contract, I can show you if you want to see it, it says I can take my six-week vacation in increments on as little as twenty-four hours' notice. I told my director Mr. Coyle that I would be gone for two weeks last Saturday shortly after the taping of an interview show I produce."

The reporter from Newark spoke up. "We're not giving you any third degree, Clark, even though you're an outrageously overpaid anchorman and you were only actually gone a week and a half and you always seem to pick up on the biggest stories around for no apparent reason except bum luck. Just kidding."

"What we would like to do, actually," this was the *London Times*'s Metropolis correspondent speaking now, "is find out precisely why it was that Superman chose you to preempt this alien potentate's planned hypnotic broadcast."

"I was the only one in the building at the time who could pass unnoticed through the news department here, and since I was just getting back from vacation, I wasn't around during the time Towbee the alien took control of the minds of everyone else here at Galaxy Broadcasting and everyone controlling TV and telephone and radio facilities all over the world. I just slipped through the alien's guard during his one weak moment. If Superman hadn't spotted me here before one of Towbee's agents did, the population of Earth might be mobilized on the way to conquer Alpha Centauri right now, and all the stars clearly visible to the naked eye at night might be physically disconnected from the gravity of the rest of the Galaxy. And Superman might be no more than a historical fact. My role in the whole thing was just that of Superman's tool to take the would-be conquerer off guard."

Lois Lane stuck her head in the door of the conference room. "Clark, it's time for you to see Mr. Edge."

"Excuse me, ladies and gentlemen, it seems I'm an important person just now."

Edge arranged for himself and Clark to tape a joint statement about the previous day's extraordinary events for showing on Galaxy Broadcasting affiliates only. Clark

233

would say how scared he was, and Edge would read telegrams from the President and the Secretary-General of the United Nations thanking Superman, wherever he was, for being a hero. First Clark and Lois had to get past Steve Lombard to the elevators.

"Hey, Clarkie, we've got a bet going. Whatcha doing for lunch, Lois?"

"Something else."

"I set it all up for after the news tonight. Jimmy Olsen, Lola Barnett, and Pelé are going to judge my Bloody Mary against your mother's wonderful soft drink. How about supper, Lois?"

"Sorry, I'm going to be busy filing my nails tonight. Why are these elevators so slow?"

"I'd ask you to have dinner with me tomorrow, Babe, but Clark's gonna owe me a banquet at Tudor's after I win the bet, aintcha, Clarkie?"

In the elevator on the way up to the 36th floor Clark felt for the little lump in his jacket pocket. It was a vial of a liquid spice for which he had traded a diamond chip on Oric. A drop of it added to a pail of mop water would make the liquid irresistible to the human palate. Imagine what it would do with the already ineffable taste of Mrs. Kent's soft drink mixture. Steve didn't have a chance. Clark had been busy making statements to police and reporters and Galaxy executives, signing papers and affidavits and that sort of nonsense since the world woke up again the night before. Superman could avoid such clerical madness simply by flying away, but Clark couldn't. Still, he declined to go home when Morgan Edge offered him the rest of the week off. Instead Edge ordered a cot set up in Clark's office and told his star anchorman to get some sleep before the broadcast of the evening news.

The most powerful man on Earth was alone at last behind the locked door of Clark Kent's office. Hidden from the world, he slid the flat leaden case out of his bottom desk drawer and ran a diamond-hard fingernail around the edge. Inside were just a few pages handwritten in Kryptonese. He read them.

Dear Kal-El,

I congratulate you on reading this message. It means that you have grown up, and almost certainly done great things with your special abilities. I must first thank your father, through you, for the remarkable gift of your Kryptonese language. The planting of knowledge in full bloom inside the brain is most stimulating, though I understand it will last only a few more days and I must not bore you with an old man's capricious discoveries.

Your father Jor-El wanted very much for you to be raised in a virtuous environment and for that reason, unknown to you, I was aware of your impending arrival on our humble Earth several hours before you landed . . .

There it was, written in Kyrptonese, in ink that had dried years before anyone on Earth, to Superman's knowledge, had ever heard of the planet Krypton. Written at a time when the very notion of life of any sort on another world—let alone life with pretensions to intelligence—was considered to be a speculative metaphor at best. And written by the possessor of the most celebrated intellect of this most fabulous century.

Einstein wrote of the exhilaration he felt at being spoken to in the Universal language of scientists, the language of mathematics, when the navigational unit transmitted mentally the trajectory of the infant Kal-El's rocket. From the information imprinted on the physicist's brain by the navigational unit's telepathic recording he was easily able to calculate the time and place of the landing. He explained:

You see, your father had the very best of intentions when he pleaded with me to raise you as my own son. I would certainly have wanted to do so, but I believe I made the right decision in simply seeing to it that you were intercepted by those fine people Jonathan and Martha Kent.

I inferred from Jor-El's telepathic message that he put great store in virtue, and also that the greatest virtue, to a Kryptonian, was intelligence. I learned that as a matter of course Krypton was ruled by a council of esteemed scientists, that the most revered individuals on your native world were those whose lives were concerned with creativity. The theorists, the artists, the poets, the inventors. It is not quite that way here on Earth, I realized. Our ethical system places kindness and honesty above all, not achievement. Simply by being who you were, your life was certain to be one of great achievement. I reasoned that if you were to grow to manhood among us it would be a much better idea for your greatest influences, your foster parents, to be individuals who were wealthy not in achievement and intellect necessarily, but in the kindness and honesty and unshakable goodness which we here on Earth have valued so highly in the scant years of our civilization.

I thought of my children as I received Jor-El's message and I gave thanks that they had a fine mother rich in those virtues. So I determined to go to Smallville as your father requested, but not to adopt you myself . . .

As he read the story of how Einstein happened upon the Kents in Sam Culler's hardware shop, the Man of Steel refused to recognize the existence of some moisture around his eyes. That was a trait he had picked up on Earth.

He realized how directly the events of his life came to this time and place. He realized that for the first time he now knew the whole story of his own life. He realized how much his father had done for him, how Jor-El had with deliberation and brilliance given the Universe a superman.

I have read that orphans like yourself are often plagued with self-doubt, wondering if their parents would really approve of the way they conduct their lives. Occasionally, I understand, people such as yourself even resent their parents for not being there to guide them. I hope that this little note helps to assuage whatever of those doubts you may feel.

For myself, I am content. I have learned that as I have always suspected, there are miraculous doings across the Universe and that there is much yet to be discovered. I confess that before your father's navigational device disintegrated several days ago I could not begin to understand its mechanism. That is just as well, it would be best for us to make our discoveries in order one at a time. I thank you for joining us on Earth, Kal-El, and I will always regard you as an almost son.

Best,
A. Einstein

The man with powers and abilities far beyond those of mortal men sometimes wondered why he was so attached to this small world and its scurrying inhabitants. In moments like these, though, he understood. Nowhere had he seen greater valor than in these four billion humans who cried as easily as they laughed, who cheated as they were cheated, who seemed bound unbreakably to a tiny clump of water and dirt careening endlessly around a dwarf star, yet dared to dream of God.

Epilogue

The scribe recorded the words of Sonnabend the prophet. Words that would be preserved for eternity by the immortal Guardians, a collection of verses to guide the righteous across the eons.

Not for billions of years, by Earth measure, would the words of the particular verses he now recorded apply. But when the time came, they would certainly prove true:

> Star Child will leave a deathworld
> For the System of the Rings;
> Where the child will grow to legend
> As his life the singer sings.

> When the conqueror wants his secret
> With the Star Child he'll contend;
> As the legend strains all glory
> An arm's freedom he'll defend.

As he recorded these particular verses a small shudder rattled the time around the scribe. . . .